HER ALIEN SPYMASTER

SUSAN HAYES

SUSAN HAYES

Her Alien Spymaster (Book 4 of the Drift: Haven Colony)

First Print & E-book Publication: July 2022

Editor: Amanda Brown

Published by: Black Scroll Publications Ltd.

DEDICATION

For my Mum and Dad, for all their love and support.

ABOUT THE BOOK

She went into cryo-sleep a prisoner and woke up free...

Skye thought freedom meant she could make her own choices. What to eat, where to live, and who she'd love. She's learning that life doesn't work that way, and fate has a mind of its own.

The cynical veteran spymaster wasn't the male she'd have chosen, but he's the one she's destined for... Except he doesn't believe she is his mate. In fact, he's certain he can't have one at all.

A spymaster lives for duty - no possessions, no attachments - and absolutely no mate.

Yardan has lived by those rules since the day he took his oath. His duty is to advise and protect Prince Tyran and Haven colony, and lately he's failed them both. He needs to redeem his honor and uncover the mole in their midst, but first he has to deal with a beautiful cyborg who insists they are destined for each other.

Skye is smart, desirable, and a distraction to his investigation. Could she also be the spy he's hunting for? Or is she something more dangerous? Like the mate he is forbidden to have...

PROLOGUE

BEYOND THE EDGE of civilized space is a newly colonized planet. It's a haven for the homeless, the hopeful, and those dreaming of freedom.

The beings who live here might be different species from vastly different worlds - but they all have one thing in common. Whoever they are, and wherever they came from, Haven is now their home.

The land is uncharted. The dangers are unknown. It's a world full of possibilities – for those willing to risk everything.

Welcome to Haven Colony.

1

SKYE RAN AS FAST as she could manage, which wasn't nearly as fast as she would have liked. The ice and snow on the ground made it impossible to reach anything close to her top speed, but the added difficulty almost made up for it. She'd come out here to burn off some energy and try to find some semblance of calm, but despite the solitude and silence of the wintery woods, she couldn't find even a moment's peace. All she could think about was the threat to Haven colony... her home.

The worst part wasn't the fact there was a threat. She was a *fraxxing* cyborg after all. She was designed from the DNA up for combat, but she had no idea how to fight against an enemy she couldn't even see. Something was sickening every Vardarian in Haven, and none of them knew if it would spread to the other species that called the colony home.

Nothing about the illness made any sense. The Vardarians were born with cutting-edge nanotech that gave them a number of advantages, including accelerated healing and the ability to cleanse their systems of any toxins or viruses. The cyborgs all carried a different kind of nanotech, which they called medi-bots, that provided the same benefits. So why were the Vardarians the only ones getting sick? And why hadn't any of the humans been infected? Most of them hadn't been given the medi-bot treatment yet. They should have been the first to fall ill.

Skye snarled in frustration and increased her pace. Two strides later, her foot hit an icy patch. She skidded, cursed, and caught hold of a tree to prevent herself from falling ass over afterburner.

"Don't get cocky," she muttered to herself. "Or in this case, don't get emotional. Emotions get you just as dead as cockiness." Then she winced. She'd just butchered one of the cyborgs' favorite mottos. Good thing none of them were around to hear what she'd said, or she would never hear the end of it. That was the problem with having cyborgs as friends and family... they never forgot a damned thing and were more than happy to bring up choice tidbits at the most annoying moments.

It's a good thing she loved the rowdy group of survivors who had made it off Reamus Station. If she didn't, she'd have dropped-kicked most of them out an airlock by now.

Once her mind and body both were balanced again, she set off at a slower pace. She enjoyed the stark beauty of the woods when it was blanketed by fluffy frozen water, but the way sound behaved in this environment intrigued her and held her attention.

The crunch and squeak of snow beneath her boots was sharp and immediate. Every exhalation seemed louder than normal, punctuated by the puffs of vapor that accompanied each breath. Other sounds were muffled by the blanket of snow. The wind blowing through the trees and the creak of branches were harder to detect despite her enhanced senses.

She let her mind wander, chasing after stray thoughts until she finally outran her worries, at least for a little while. She'd needed this.

After another few kilometers, she circled back, breaking a new trail instead of following her previous tracks. Her new route would eventually take her to the bridge that linked the two sides of the colony, but it also took her through one of her favorite spots, a wide meadow with a stream running through it. It had been covered in soft green and blue grass with wildflowers the first time she'd seen it. Now, it looked very different. The wind had blown the snow into drifts that looked like frozen waves, piling it up against the trunks of trees along the far side of the field. She saw tracks here and there, most of them from small animals, but something larger had been through here since the last snowfall.

She jogged over and looked at the prints, trying to discern what might have made them. Striker would know, but she didn't want to disturb the big, somewhat grumpy cyborg. They were friends now, but she'd been wary of him at one time. She understood him better now, but that didn't mean she was ready to call him on their internal channels and have a chat about the tracks left by the local wildlife.

Besides, the antisocial cyborg usually had his channels switched off. "What Maggie sees in him I will never understand. When I'm ready to settle down, I'll find someone cheerful, all charm and sass. Yeah." She glanced up at the sky. "That comment was not a request for said male to arrive just yet. I'm still enjoying my freedom, thank you very much."

She'd picked up the habit from the human colonists. Most of them believed in one higher being or another, and all of them seemed to look up when they were communicating with them.

She stayed in the field long enough to enjoy the tranquility and capture a few images of the tracks with her onboard optics. Given their size, it had to be either a ghost cat or a *kopaki*. Both were large predators that had developed a taste for the colony's assorted species of livestock. She'd have to let the rangers know what she'd seen. They'd take care of it once the more immediate crisis was over.

That thought shattered her moment of peace. "I'd

take a pack of ghost cats over this damned bug. At least then I'd have something to hit."

She was halfway back when River pinged her over their shared channel. "Skye, I've got an update."

"I'm listening."

"I heard from Maggie. Since the council can't get anything done, we're going a different way. I'm rounding up everyone here and taking them to the Bar None. Meet you there?"

It was the best news she'd heard in days. "I'm already running. Let's see who gets there first."

Skye turned and took off at the fastest speed she could manage. She had no chance of beating River and the others to the bar, but she wouldn't be far behind them. They were going to do *something*, and that was all she needed to know.

At this time of day, the bridge was usually humming with activity. Haven's citizens should be socializing and shopping at the various vendors and market stalls that lined the street, linking the two sides of the colony. Today, though, it was silent and empty. All the shops and stalls were shuttered, and the only sound she heard was the rush of water beneath her feet and the occasional crash as chunks of ice slammed into each other.

She was well onto the bridge before she heard

voices. It was no surprise they came from the Bar None. The meeting must be underway already. *Good.*

She spotted River's vehicle parked nearby. A quick scan showed the engine hadn't started cooling yet. She wasn't far behind them. She knocked the snow from her boots and opened the door. A rush of warm, richly scented air wafted by as she stepped into one of the most comfortable places she knew.

The building wasn't even a year old yet, but somehow this place already felt older and more broken in. Entering the bar was like slipping into her favorite pair of boots. She'd barely crossed the threshold when everyone else erupted into excited cheers.

Hope bloomed, and she raised her voice to be heard above the others. "Does this mean we have a plan?"

The only male present rose from his seat. She recognized him immediately and wondered what the *fraxx* he was doing here. The prince's spymaster was dour and distrustful, especially when it came to the non-Vardarian citizens of Haven.

She expected him to say something to dampen the mood or point out something they'd all overlooked. Instead, his golden skin lost most of its luster as he crashed to the floor.

Shit.

Phaedra was at his side in a second, concern shadowing her normally sunny expression. "You stubborn *fraxxing*, idiot. You didn't tell me you were sick, too."

Well, that explained what the spymaster was doing here. He didn't have much love for humans, but Phaedra was the prince's mate. She was also stubborn, impulsive, and resistant to authority. Since her bodyguards weren't present, Yardan had come instead. Phaedra must have loved that.

Yardan waved everyone off. "I'm not sick. I just got up too fast."

Skye scanned him. He had an elevated temperature, a rapid pulse, and several other indicators of illness.

Stubborn fraxxing idiot indeed, she thought and walked over to help him up. She hadn't intended to do that, but she was halfway there before she even realized she was moving.

He glared at her for a few seconds, just long enough for her to wonder if he'd refuse her assistance, but then he took her hand in his and tried to pull himself up.

Skye saw him struggling and simply lifted him off the floor, using her enhanced strength to get him on his feet. That's when it hit her... a subtle rush of warmth and desire. Oh *fraxx*, no. Him? Now? This couldn't be the *sharhal*. Surely she'd been close enough to him before today... Her mind raced as she accessed her memory, cross-referencing every time she'd encountered the spymaster or his *anrik*. Wait. Did he even have one? She checked his wrist for the scar that every other Vardarian male wore with pride. His skin was smooth. No scar. No *anrik*. No blood-brother to journey through life with. That meant if this was what she thought it was, she wouldn't be the filling in a sexy male sandwich. *Pity.*

By the time she'd worked through that, though, her memory cross-check confirmed that the two of them had never been inside the few times they'd attended at the same functions, and they'd never been introduced.

Typical. Her *mahoyen* had been here all along, and she'd never crossed paths with him until today. She managed a sidelong look at him as he leaned against her. His hair and beard were both dark and closely trimmed, framing a handsome face with a strong jaw and green eyes that glittered with intelligence edged in ice.

Grumpy but good looking—she could work with that.

She draped one of his well-muscled arms over her shoulders and caught him around his waist with the other. "I got you," she told him as she drew his hard body in close to her side.

He shot her a disgruntled look. "Apparently. Damned females shouldn't be that strong. And I'm fine."

Phaedra chimed in before Skye could. "He's not close to fine. Can you help me get him home?"

A moment ago all she wanted was to take on the

threat to Haven and find a way to help her adopted home. Strange how quickly things could change. She glanced at Yardan and then nodded. If she was right and they were destined to be mates, she would go with him. Besides, Phaedra would need help running things while both of her mates were down with whatever the *fraxx* this plague was. "You can fill me in on what's happening on the way."

"Suki, grab our coats. Will you?" Phaedra asked one of the human colonists. Then she picked up Yardan's heavy cloak from the back of his chair and managed to toss it over his shoulders. Phae was too short to place it carefully, so Skye took a moment to adjust it before helping the spymaster outside.

Skye kept expecting him to say something about the *sharhal*. The Vardarian should be feeling the effects even more than she was. So why hadn't he said anything? She'd been prepared for the possibility that she'd end up mated to a Vardarian. From what she'd seen, it wasn't so bad. Hell, it was probably better this way. Dating wasn't something the survivors of Reamus Station knew much about. She'd enjoyed a few no-strings-attached encounters here in Haven, but that wasn't the same.

She glanced over at Yardan again. All his attention was on Phaedra, walking a few steps ahead of them. Just her *fraxxing* luck. She finally met her destined mate, and he was too sick to notice her.

Once he was healthy, things would be different.

They had to be. Otherwise, she was in trouble. Once triggered, the Vardarian mating fever couldn't be stopped. Either she'd wind up mated or she'd lose herself to madness and death.

She knew which option she'd prefer. The rest was up to Yardan.

2

Being sick was a new experience for Yardan, and he wasn't enjoying it. In fact, it was one of the most humiliating trials of his life. He was as weak as a newborn, and his mind refused to focus. Worst of all, he needed to rely on other beings to help him until his strength returned. It stung his pride.

So did the memory of the cyborg female carrying him out of the Bar None. The recollection was fever-blurred and fractured, but he remembered enough to know that while he'd pretended she was merely supporting him, the truth was she'd barely let his feet touch the ground.

He was grateful to her for not revealing just how weak he was, but he chafed at the thought that he now owed her for that sop to his already battered pride. He was the prince's trusted advisor, the one who unearthed every secret threat and stamped it out before it could take root. Not only had he failed to detect this attack, but he'd fallen victim to it himself, just like every other Vardarian in the colony.

He should have done more.

A whisper of sound somewhere to his left told him he wasn't alone in his room. He didn't have to open his eyes to know Skye was nearby. She'd stayed close ever since they'd returned to the prince's modest palace.

He turned his head in the direction of the noise, opened his eyes, and asked, "How is Prince Tyran faring?"

Skye lounged in a chair near his bedside, her long legs stretched out in front of her. Despite her easy demeanor, she was alert to everything going on outside this room. He recognized the way she moved... it was like looking in a mirror. They'd both been conditioned to never lower their guard.

"Almost as grumpy as you are, but he's recovering quickly. You would be too if you'd taken the injection when it was first offered," she said wryly.

He took a moment to appreciate how pretty his visitor was. Her hair was somewhere between blonde and brown, darker now than it had been during the summer when the tips had been bleached by the sun. He'd seen her from a distance more than once, but they'd never spoken until yesterday. He had too much to do, and his position did not allow for distractions of any kind, especially not pretty females. A spymaster had but one purpose, and his loyalty to the one he served had to be absolute.

"I should have been given it first to ensure it was safe. Since no one thought to ask me, I saw no reason to put my need before that of the others in the prince's service."

She snorted. "You could just admit you were sulking because no one consulted you."

"I do not sulk. It would be beneath my station to behave in such a way."

"Uh huh." She gazed at him with eyes as blue as a summer sky. "I have spent my entire life surrounded by men who never want to admit to feeling emotions. You don't need to pretend with me."

He ignored her blunt statement to ask the question foremost in his mind since the first time he'd awoken to find her in his room. "Why are you even here?"

Her smile really was beguiling. It softened her features and made her seem approachable despite the fact she was taller than most females and far more deadly. The cyborgs of the colony were all from the same research station, and every one of them had been deemed too dangerous to be allowed off-world. For someone like that to have taken on the role of his personal nurse didn't sit right with him.

"Where else would I be?" she asked.

Answering a question with another question was one of his tricks, and he didn't enjoy having it turned around on him. "That isn't an answer."

She cocked her head, her blue eyes twinkling now, as if waiting for him to grasp the punchline of some joke he'd missed. "You haven't noticed yet? Breathe deeply, Yardan. Tell me what you smell."

He inhaled. His sense of smell was limited, but he could still pick up most odors if he focused. The scent of home cooking, the spikey tang of a suspect's fear... and even a whisper of something that shouldn't have been in his rooms—the scent of a female.

He shook his head. "I don't smell anything unusual, but that's not surprising. I haven't had full use of that sense in more years than I care to admit."

Her smile flickered and then died. "What? Nothing? Why not?"

Yardan sat up, some sense whispering to him that this conversation was more important than he currently understood. At least he had recovered enough that his mind was clear. "I am the prince's *Naram T'kar*. You would call me his spymaster. The day I finished my training and made my vows, I did what all the others before me have done."

He rolled his shoulders to rid himself of the stiffness that lingered because he'd been too long in this damned bed. "My position requires sacrifice. Tradition states that a *Naram T'kar* can have no distractions. I have no *anrik*. I severed ties with my family and friends. I gave up what few possessions I had, and the healers adjusted my senses so I will never be tempted by the greatest distraction of all."

"What would that be?" Skye's tone held a brittle edge now, and something wary and sad flickered in her lovely eyes. He had no idea why she was upset. That piece of the puzzle still eluded him. What was he missing?

He touched his nose. "If I were to find my *mahaya*, I could not fulfill my duty. So the healers made adjustments to my body to ensure I cannot detect those pheromones. It affects my sense of smell and taste, too, but not completely."

"But how would that work? Even if you can't sense your mate, I—she could sense you."

He shook his head. "The ancestors set me on this path. I have no *mahaya*. But even if I did, the healers ensured I would never give off the pheromone that would attract a female."

Skye rose to her feet, tension crackling off her now. "You're wrong about that."

By all the winds that blew, she really was beautiful. Why hadn't one of the cyborg males claimed her already? Were they blind? For the first time since taking his vows, he heard the smallest whisper of temptation... and promptly squashed it like a bug beneath his boot. "I am not wrong. This is my purpose. This is the life the ancestors set out for me when I was still a boy."

She scowled at him. "Your ancestors got it wrong, then."

He didn't understand. "What did they get wrong?"

"You do have a *mahaya*, Yardan."

"That's not possible."

Her expression turned unhappy. "Then why have I been feeling the pull of the *sharhal* since I picked you up off that floor?"

"No. You can't be. I cannot have a mate."

"You're wrong."

"You don't understand. This isn't possible." It couldn't be. Not unless the ancestors had taken leave of their senses... or he wasn't supposed to be Tyran's spymaster anymore. Was he to be stripped of his position for failing to protect the prince? Was this some sort of karmic punishment?

"You know, if you keep telling me I'm wrong and that you can't have a mate, I'm going to start taking it personally."

He scrubbed a hand over his close-cropped hair and tried to find some words that weren't going to make this situation worse. "It's not you. You're lovely. Truly. Any male would be lucky to claim you as his own. But I'm not that male. I can't be."

"You keep saying that." She walked over and put a callused hand on his cheek. "But you're wrong."

The touch of her hand felt better than anything he'd ever known. Tender. Gentle. Right.

He turned his head and brushed her hand away with his. "Stop saying I'm wrong, female. This is not happening."

"Oh, it is." She let her fingers graze over his cheek

as she moved away. "If you don't believe me now, that's fine. I'll go to your healers and have them confirm it. Then I'm coming back here. You have until then to come to terms with this."

A tiny whisper of suspicion sounded at the back of his mind. "You seem to be adjusting quite well to the idea of being bound to a stranger. Most humans take longer."

She winked at him. "I'm not human, though. I'm a cyborg. And after everything I've already survived in my life, this doesn't scare me at all. I've been to hell and back so many times I know the way blindfolded."

"And if I say no?" The words were out before he could stop himself. He knew what would happen if he denied her this claim. If it was real, that is. She'd suffer pain, madness, and possibly death.

"If you say no, that's your choice to make. I'd rather go back to hell again than take another being's choices away from them. I know too well how that feels."

He didn't know what to say to that, so he said nothing.

"I need to say one more thing, and then I'll go." She drew a breath and looked him in the eyes. "Being stubborn is not the same as being right."

She blew him a kiss and departed, leaving him alone with dozens of questions and no answers.

Was the beautiful cyborg a planned distraction, a punishment... or his reward? He had no idea. The only thing he could be certain of was that the answers to his questions weren't in his room. He'd have to go looking for them.

It took longer than he liked to shower and dress, but he managed it without succumbing to the fatigue that had dogged him since he'd been infected with Helix Fever. If he had his way, none of his people would ever experience that kind of misery again. Falling ill had been one of the worst experiences of his life, and the humans considered it a minor ailment. *Minor*. How had humans managed to achieve so much when they were so qarfing vulnerable?

He already knew the answer. They were resourceful, cunning, and deceitful, even to their own kind. Skye had kept him updated while he recovered, replacing the reports he should have received from his network. He only relied on Vardarians, which proved problematic when most of them had been afflicted by the illness, too. He would have to expand his network, even if that meant trusting some of the other citizens of Haven. The thought made the scales on the back of his neck tighten. Trust wasn't something he did well.

He snorted in derision and refolded his wings into a more comfortable position. If he was being honest, trust wasn't something he did much of, period. His position made him the master of dangerous secrets, ones he could only entrust to the prince and a few others. This was why those elevated to his position couldn't have relationships. Along with the fact that with every new connection came the risk they could be used against him, either as a mole or a hostage.

Skye had to be wrong. Either she wasn't experiencing the *sharhal,* or she was actually destined for someone else and had misread her attraction. Only the latter meant that a Vardarian had caught the scent of his *mahaya* and let her slip away. If they had, he was an utter fool. He and his *anrik* would no doubt be looking for her already. If that was the case, he wished them good luck. Whoever her mates were, they would need it.

He would have someone look into how things unfolded for Skye later today. For now, he needed to speak with the prince.

He had apologies to make... and plans to discuss.

3

———

A QUICK INQUIRY with one of the palace guards gave him the prince's current location. He was in his office, working. No surprise there. Tyran took his duty as seriously as his father once had. The prince would have made a fine emperor. Yardan sometimes wondered what their lives would be like if Tyran had been born before his twin sister. Neha was a decent ruler, but her brother...

He shook the thought out of his head before he approached the prince's door. Matters were as they were. Wishing differently was a waste of time and energy, and right now he didn't have enough of either.

The guard saw him coming and saluted. He rapped on the door and announced Yardan's arrival while he was still several steps away.

"Send him in," Tyran called out.

The guard opened the door and gestured him inside. "Good to see you back on your feet, sir."

Yardan nodded in acknowledgment. "Thank you, Lavis."

The prince sat behind his desk with Braxon seated to one side. Yardan had expected to find the prince's *anrik* here, but he had assumed their mate would be off doing… whatever females did when they were with child. Resting? Eating strange combinations of food? He wasn't really sure, but he hadn't expected to encounter Phaedra here.

Tyran rose to greet him, and Yardan noted that the prince moved slower than usual. So, he wasn't completely recovered yet either. That worried him. They were all vulnerable right now, and he still had no idea how to stop another such attack.

"Yardan. I thought you were supposed to rest for another day." Tyran greeted him with a warm smile. "Though I have to admit, I'm glad to see you. We have things to discuss."

"Yes, my prince." Yardan saluted and then nodded to Braxon and Phaedra. Phaedra grinned and leaned over as if trying to see behind him. "Where's Skye? Did you ditch your *mahaya* to go back to work?"

Tyran and Braxon both whipped their heads around to stare at Yardan.

"Skye?" one asked.

"*Mahaya?*" the other said.

Yardan glowered but managed not to growl at the

perky, pink-haired human his prince had claimed as his mate. "She is not my *mahaya*. I am the *Naram T'kar* of the royal family. I cannot have a mate."

"Uh huh." Phae sat back in her chair. "That's not what Skye thinks."

He waved the comment away. "She is wrong."

Phaedra tapped a finger to her lips and stayed silent, but her eyes glittered with amusement.

Tyran gestured to an empty chair and then took a seat. "I think we should leave that topic for another time. For now, I want to hear your thoughts on what was done to us."

"And how to make sure it never happens again," Braxon chimed in.

"Agreed." Yardan sat down and summarized what he knew. "As unpleasant as it was, the Helix Fever outbreak was the only way we learned what else had been done to us. We'll need to come up with ways to monitor our nanotech going forward. I'll discuss this with the healers. We can't be caught off guard this way again."

"We won't be," Tyran stated, his tone firm. "Whatever our enemies had planned for us, they failed. First, someone attempted to convert Kade D'vrayn into an intelligence asset. Then a group hired mercenaries to capture one of our citizens in order to recover proof that they were slipping spies into the colony. Now this." The prince looked directly at Yardan. "They're getting bolder."

Yardan nodded. "Yes, they are. Forgive me for pointing this out, but so far you have only referred to this group as our enemy. That isn't accurate."

Phaedra's lips pursed, but he ignored her displeasure and continued. "We believe the attempt to recruit Kade D'vrayn was made for a human corporation called Torex. The mercenaries who came after Maggie were sent by humans. So was Kara, the human spy planted among the first colonists from Earth. We know who the enemy is. They're humans."

"Did you just lump an entire species together and blame us all for the actions of an assholish few?" Phaedra scowled and jerked a thumb toward her chest. "I spent most of my life fighting against people like that. Humans aren't the problem, Spymaster. The corporations are."

His translator glitched on the word assholish, but Yardan had spent enough time around the princess to grasp her meaning. He also acknowledged that the female had a valid point. With a pained sigh, he bowed his head to Phaedra. "The corporations, yes. *Those* humans are our problem... and our enemy."

She blinked at him in obvious surprise. "Yes. Uh, thank you."

"Are you feeling alright?" Braxon asked.

"I'm fine. Why do you ask?"

"Because that's the first time I've ever heard you change your stance without a prolonged argument first," Phaedra said.

"In this case, I misspoke." He looked first at Tyran and then let his gaze move back to Phaedra. "Recently, it has been pointed out to me that I have been resistant to change, even when it is to the detriment of the colony." He allowed his lips to lift into a brief smile. "I will try to be more aware of that in the future."

Phaedra laughed, and he heard real joy in the sound. It made him realize how long it had been since he'd heard anyone laugh like that in his presence. Not that he saw many beings. His line of work generally kept him secluded.

Tyran shifted in his chair and resettled his wings with enough noise and motion to capture the attention of everyone present. "Now that we have agreed on who our enemy is, we need to prepare for their next attack."

Yardan nodded and then leaned forward in his chair. "We must also find the spies still in our midst. The female, Kara, claimed she was approached while on Earth by a human male." He paused for a brief moment until he recalled the male's name. "Grayson."

Phaedra stiffened. "We have his name? This is news to me. I've been too busy to keep up with all the reports coming in. Grayson..." She chewed on her lower lip and then sighed. "Do you think he's one of the Gray Men?"

This was the problem with translators. Some concepts and words lost their connection to each other in the process. He hadn't connected the male's surname with the word for a color, or the shadowy cabal that still managed to survive despite continuous attempts to annihilate them.

Grim silence followed as everyone processed that possibility.

Tyran sighed. "It makes sense."

Phaedra chimed in. "And it also explains why Nova Force is sending a team here for Kara. They want to interrogate her."

It was Yardan's turn to frown. "Nova Force is coming here? Why wasn't I informed?"

"Because this news only reached us an hour ago, and you are still supposed to be resting," Tyran said.

"I'm tired of resting. I need to work," Yardan grumbled. "And Skye never mentioned I was supposed to stay in bed."

Braxon's brow lifted at the mention of the cyborg female, but he didn't say anything.

Tyran paused long enough that Yardan braced himself for unpleasant news. Finally, he looked at the prince and sighed. "What aren't you telling me?"

"Lieutenant Jessop requested permission to interview the suspect while you were still unconscious. I gave it to her."

"You allowed someone else access to our best source of information? One of..." He stopped himself before he said the word on the tip of his tongue. *Them.*

"One of our allies, yes. Aria Jessop is one of the best interrogators in Nova Force. You said so yourself," Tyran reminded him.

"I did, and she is. I am just not used to being sidelined like this." He looked at Phaedra. "How does your species manage so well with ailments like this?"

"We don't have any other choice, or we didn't until recently. It's amazing what you can accept if you don't think there's any other way."

He made a note of that comment. It summarized the humans' mentality in a way that helped him understand them better. Enemy or ally, he needed to know their thought processes and what drove them to do the things they did.

In many ways the lieutenant was in the same work as he was, but Yardan hadn't spoken more than a few words to her. She was here in Haven for personal reasons, and the cyborgs helping her had made it clear that she needed to focus on her recovery. He'd respected that. She'd lost her leg during an op and had come to the colony to learn how to adjust to life as a cyborg.

It still surprised him how fragile humans were. At least the ones who had yet to take the nanotech treatment, which brought up another issue.

"The remaining human colonists. I take it that after this, they'll all be granted full citizenship and access to the nanotech?"

"They earned it," Phaedra stated and gave him a look that dared him to argue with her.

He waved her off. "I agree. They are also

vulnerable without the protection that technology provides."

"You have no concerns that more spies may be in their ranks?" Braxon asked.

"Oh, I have more than a few concerns, but most, if not all of them, are exactly what they claim to be. Denying them the tech serves no purpose." And once they joined the main colony, it would be easier for him to keep a watchful eye over them. Skye and the others tasked with helping the colonists transition to their new lives had already failed to detect one spy. He couldn't trust them not to make the same mistake again.

By the time they had plans in place, all of them showed signs of fatigue. Phaedra had pushed herself hard while her mates were ill, and she needed rest even more than they did.

He met Tyran's eyes, and the prince nodded once in understanding before sitting back in his chair. "I think we're done for now. As much as I hate to admit this, I am not fully recovered. We should all retire for the evening before the healers descend and nag us into submission."

"Agreed. With your permission, I'll be on my way." He rose and then paused. "I'll formally launch my investigation tomorrow. My first act will be to interview the spy while she's still in our custody. Any word on when Nova Force will arrive to take custody?"

"Team Two is already enroute. They were in the

area, galactically speaking, and will arrive in a matter of days. I'll make sure you're sent all updates on their arrival time," Tyran said.

"Thank you."

He was on his way back to his office a few minutes later, already sorting through the myriad of pieces to this complex and still incomplete puzzle. Sleep would have to wait. He had work to do.

4

———

Skye hadn't left the palace grounds since she'd brought Phaedra and Yardan here. That had been—she had to think for a moment—two days ago. *Veth*. Only two days? She checked her onboard systems to confirm it. That's all it had been, but a quick review told her in that time she'd only managed an hour of sleep. Even her medi-bots couldn't keep her on her feet forever. Now the height of the crisis had passed, she needed to rest.

That thought should have sent her homeward. Instead, she opted for a different route, one that led to one of the smaller med-clinics. For now, Haven only had Vardarian healers. It was one of the reasons they'd had so much trouble diagnosing the fever that tore through the colony. Once the council was well enough to meet again, they'd have to rectify that oversight.

She sighed and tipped her face up toward the night

sky, watching the snowflakes drift and swirl downward. She'd never experienced weather until she'd awoken on this world, and while she wasn't overly enthralled with rain, snow fascinated her. Something as mundane as frozen water shouldn't be so beautiful. Flakes landed on her cheeks and lashes, the delicate crystals melting back into water moments after contact. Something was poetic about that, and she'd think about it more when she wasn't groggy and annoyed at a certain stubborn spymaster who thought he knew better than she did.

He's wrong. She knew it. He had to be wrong because she'd never felt this way before. She hadn't even known she could feel like this. Just the thought of him made her pulse rise and her skin heat. She'd told everyone she would stay at the palace to help Phaedra deal with the crisis, but that hadn't been the whole truth.

Phae had figured out what was going on by the end of the first day. By then, Skye was certain she'd needed someone to talk to. Someone who'd been through what she was dealing with. The *sharhal.*

Talking with Phaedra helped her understand what was happening and what would come next. At least, she'd thought so... but nothing had prepared her for Yardan's denial. Despite what she'd said before leaving him, she wasn't sure what the *fraxx* to do now. His rejection hurt, too. She knew he had trust issues when it came to the other races, but she hadn't expected him to be so dismissive of the situation... or of her.

Yardan didn't want to believe her, but he couldn't argue once she presented him with proof from his own healers. Sleep would have to wait a little longer.

She reached the med-clinic in a matter of minutes. She walked through the door and looked around to see if she was alone. The waiting area was empty. Not a surprise. The Vardarians were mostly at home, recovering from the fever, and the cyborgs only needed medical treatment for serious injuries. Their medi-bots took care of everything else.

Skye snorted in amusement. Well, almost everything. Apparently the *sharhal* was an exception—and so was she.

A soft, almost musical tone sounded followed by the arrival of the on-site medical hologram. Every med-clinic had one, and they were all identical—a silver-skinned, soft-spoken Vardarian female with a kind smile.

"Welcome. Please identify yourself and briefly explain why you are here."

"Skye. Um, I'm a cyborg. I've been interacting with another version of you at the palace for the last two days. I'm in need of medical advice."

The hologram smiled and nodded. "File obtained. Please follow me into an exam room and we'll proceed." She turned and gestured for Skye to follow her. "How is Yardan? I believe you have been overseeing his recovery."

The question startled her. "He's recovering quickly, though I'm sure you know that already."

"I do, but I have learned it is beneficial to seek the opinions of others in order to enhance my own observations."

Skye followed the hologram into one of the exam rooms. The air was crisp and clean with a trace of antiseptic and cleanser, as if the servo-droids had cleaned this room only a moment before. Who knew, maybe they had.

The medical holo didn't speak until the door closed, ensuring privacy. Skye appreciated the programming. The last thing she wanted was for someone else to arrive and overhear what she had to say next.

"Please tell me what advice you are seeking today."

"I think I'm experiencing the *sharhal*, but the other party is certain that isn't possible because he can't have a mate. I'm sure it's him, though." She paused for a second before adding, "I need to know which one of us is wrong."

"I believe I can answer that question once I see the results of a blood test. Do I have your permission to examine you and perform a few tests?"

Skye nodded and sat down next to a medical droid. It made her skin crawl to be this close to something so similar to the machines that had tormented her during her years on Reamus Research Station. That place still haunted her nightmares. Her life back then had been nothing but pain, abuse, and outright torture from the moment she'd left her maturation tank until she'd woken up here on the planet Liberty.

The tests were quick and painless with each procedure explained by the soothing, gender-neutral voice of the droid. The hologram asked her a few questions about her general health and well-being, which Skye suspected were more of a distraction than anything official. These centers were set up with medical scanning and diagnostic systems that would have started work the moment she gave her permission to be tested.

"Do you have a name?" she asked the hologram once the tests were done. The droid had retreated to its corner, all its various limbs folded in around itself.

The hologram nodded. "I do. You may call me Rae."

"You're based on a real being. Aren't you?" She'd heard rumors about this, but since they had a few moments, she decided to ask.

"I am. My personality and appearance were based on a Vardarian female named Raenia. She programmed me to act as an assistant to her *mahoyen*."

The hologram's expression turned almost sad for a moment. "My creator is no longer alive, but I continue to serve her family."

"You're modeled on Vixi's mother. Aren't you?" She named the young healer who had worked tirelessly through the recent crisis. Her fathers, Tariq and Sulat, were the lead healers of the entire colony.

The hologram bowed her head briefly. "I am."

"Forgive me for saying this, but that must be complicated for Tariq and his family."

Rae smiled and tipped her head to one side. "Sometimes. But I have offered to alter my appearance, and they wish me to remain like this."

Skye thought about the ones who had died before they were finally found and freed. Their memories were stored in her database, perfect and protected from the degradations of time. The Vardarians had nanotech, but they weren't cyborgs. Their memories would fade. Maybe this was their way of keeping the memory of their beloved mate fresh.

The part of her that had learned so much about counseling and healing since coming here whispered that it might also be something else. They weren't ready to let their loved one go.

Rae turned the conversation back to Skye after that, making general inquiries about her health and her observations about the recovery of the colony.

"I thought you'd have all this on file already," Skye said. "I mean, you're all connected. Aren't you?"

"Actually, we are one and the same. My system is fully networked to every med-center in the colony."

"Your system is big enough for that kind of processing power?" She wasn't an expert in computer systems, but even she knew that kind of setup would be challenging.

"It is."

A thought struck Skye. "Wait. If you can be so many places at once, why weren't you present at the arena where we brought the sick?"

"Because my network was limited to the centers and the palace. So is most of the medical equipment."

"I bet that's going to change," Skye muttered. The Vardarians were so advanced in many ways, but they'd come to rely on their technological advances to the point they took them for granted. The arenas were designed to be converted into emergency shelters, but no one had thought to network in the medical system.

"Indeed it is. Portable versions of the droids and equipment are already being designed, and my network will be extended to include emergency shelters throughout the colony."

"You mean both sides of the river?" When they'd first arrived, the colony had been split in two with the Vardarians on one riverbank and the cyborgs on the other. The two sides hadn't interacted much until the arrival of the first human colonists had spurred moving the cyborgs out of their original area to live side by side with their Vardarian neighbors.

"Both sides. We are one colony, after all."

Even the hologram gets it... so why doesn't Yardan?

"That we are," Skye agreed.

A tri-toned chime sounded, and Rae lifted her

head. "Ah, your results are in. Congratulations, Skye, you are experiencing the first stages of the *sharhal*. Though it appears to be progressing slower than normal, which is unusual."

That wasn't a word she wanted to hear right now. "Does that mean he was right and I'm not his *mahaya?* Did I somehow get it wrong?"

"Before we continue, I'll need to ask for the names of the males involved. That might simplify matters."

"Yardan..." Skye trailed off as she realized she didn't know if the spymaster had a second name. "The prince's spymaster. I don't think he has an *anrik*."

For a moment, the hologram went so still Skye thought it had glitched.

"That isn't possible."

"That he doesn't have an anrik, or that Yardan is my mate?" Skye tried to keep frustration from sharpening her tone, but she wasn't entirely successful.

"Yardan, the one you call the prince's spymaster, has been medically modified to prevent him from creating or sensing the pheromones that trigger the *sharhal*."

She threw her hands up. "That's what he said, too, but I know what I'm feeling."

"And my tests validate your feelings. You *are* experiencing the mating fever."

She felt like screaming or maybe laughing. Probably a little of both. "So either I'm wrong or he's wrong. Which is it?"

Rae lifted one hand in a shrug-like gesture. "There is another possibility, but I will need time to investigate this further."

Skye rose from the chair and stood across from the hologram. "Care to give me a hint?"

"I think it's possible you are both right."

"Before you said that wasn't possible."

"I may have been wrong about that. Please give me some time to work on this. I will contact you as soon as I have any news."

"And what do I do until then? I'm going through the mating fever without a mate. I know that's dangerous. How long do I have before this becomes a problem?" The *sharhal* couldn't be stopped. She knew that much. Those who lost their mates during this period or who couldn't complete the bond suffered intense physical and emotional torment. Some went mad from it, and others died. She'd had her share of suffering and torment already, thank you very much. She didn't need to sign up for anymore.

The hologram froze again. This time she knew it wasn't a glitch, so she just waited while the program did... whatever it was doing.

Less than a minute later, Rae was back. "I apologize for the delay. I needed to confirm several data points." The hologram folded her hands in front of her and smiled encouragingly. "There is a way to slow down the *sharhal*."

Skye gawked. That was not what she'd expected to hear. "How?"

"This procedure is technically illegal to perform except in the direst of circumstances and only with approval from both doctors and the empress. However, that law only applies to Vardarians."

The healer hologram knew how to use loopholes. Skye wasn't sure how she felt about that, but right now, she didn't care if the AI was close to violating the Pinocchio Protocol that regulated artificial intelligences. "Is it safe? I mean, for humans?"

"I would not expose you to danger, Skye. That would run counter to my programming."

"And this will slow the whole thing down?"

"It will. I cannot give you a precise timeframe, but it should provide you with two or three days before the mating fever progresses beyond what you're currently experiencing. There is a caveat, however."

"Of course there is. What's the price?" Skye asked.

"When the *sharhal* re-manifests it will be... intense."

"Noted. Do it."

"Please take a seat. I have already begun manufacturing the necessary injection."

"Will this get you into trouble?"

"My purpose is to heal those in my care. You are in a unique situation, and I have the means to help you."

Skye gave the program bonus points for concocting the best non-answer she'd heard in a while, but opted not to comment. She had bigger problems to deal with. At the top of the list was convincing Yardan she was right.

"I don't suppose there's a way to check Yardan for signs of the *sharhal*. Is there?" Skye asked as she waited.

"I cannot take samples without his permission."

She frowned and tapped a finger to her chin as she considered the situation. "Did you perform any tests on the spymaster while he was sick?" She knew it had been done because she'd been in the room when it happened, but she needed to be careful how she handled this.

The hologram nodded. "I did. Thank you for reminding me."

Skye wondered just how autonomous this AI was... and how much of its designer's personality was woven into its programing. Her oblique suggestion that the system test a previous sample rested squarely in the middle of the gray area of medical ethics, but the program had picked up on it immediately. She made a note to ask Phaedra about it later.

Neither of them said anything else. A bot scooted into the room through a small hatch near the floor and delivered an injector to the medical droid. She pulled up her sleeve. With a hiss and a brief sting, it was over.

She tugged her sleeve into place and rose from the chair. "We done?"

"We have one other matter to address before you

leave. Two, actually." The hologram smiled. "The first one is this. You need rest. After this, you are under medical orders to go home, consume something light but nutritious, and get some sleep."

"That was my plan. What's the other thing?"

"Yardan is also experiencing the mating fever, though it is far less powerful than normal. I suspect that is due to the procedures he underwent when he took on his current role. I will inform him of this in the morning."

Skye raised a hand. "I'd like to be there when you break the news."

Rae nodded sagely. "Of course. I will be in touch. Until then, get some rest."

Outside, the snow had stopped and the clouds had thinned enough that her walk home was illuminated by moonlight as much as street lights. A sense of contented calm filled her, and she nodded to herself. She knew what that meant. It was always calm... right before a storm.

5

—————

It felt good to be back in his office and ready to *do* something. The fever had left his body drained and his mind groggy, but he couldn't lie around and wait to get better.

His mother's voice sounded in his head as clearly as if she was standing beside him. "The winds of fortune only lift the wings of those brave enough to fly high and far in search of them. If you want something, my son, you must chase after it and hope the winds favor you."

He took his mother's advice and threw himself into his work. Time flew by on silent wings, and by the time he was satisfied he'd made a good start, it was only a few hours before dawn.

Unlike most of his people, Yardan didn't use an AI assistant for anything but the most mundane of tasks, like reminding him of meetings and ensuring he always had a mug of something that would keep his mind sharp. He'd recently discovered that humans combined coffee and cocoa into something they called a mocha. It was his current favorite, and he stood back to assess what he'd accomplished while sipping a fresh cup.

Holographic displays filled his office. Some of them listed names, others locations, yet another showed the timeline of events as he currently understood them. Somewhere in this mass of data was the information he needed to catch their spy. Now came the slow part— eliminating everything not pertinent to the case until all that was left was the truth.

His gaze flicked to the list of names. He'd included all but a few humans, a number of cyborgs, and a handful of Vardarians. Not that he suspected any of his people were part of this. They were dealing with a human enemy, and Vardarians were a new arrival to this part of the galaxy. Their adversary hadn't had enough time to recruit from his species. Instinct told him it was one of the cyborgs. And that meant all of them were suspects... including Skye.

He took another sip of his drink and sighed, suddenly tired. This part had always been the hardest for him, but it was also the reason why all *Naram T'kar* kept themselves isolated from everyone else. It was their job to suspect everyone... always.

He woke just an hour after his usual time, and the moment he got to his feet, he felt the difference. He was fully recovered, or as close to it as to make no difference.

"Welcome back," he muttered and patted his own chest. He wasn't young by the standards of his people, but he wasn't old either. He still had a century or two left before the nanotech would allow the aging process to begin. Now that he'd had a taste of what that might feel like, he wasn't looking forward to it. But his species had long since learned that eternal life caused more harm than good. Society stagnated, population control became a problem, and their minds weren't designed to process centuries of memories and emotions.

He fell into his old routine quite happily. He showered, trimmed his beard, dressed in a pair of loose-fitting pants, and then went outside to start his day. The only difference was the mug of mocha he carried.

The palace grounds were stark and white with snow that reflected the morning sunlight and made everything so bright he winced. The crisp, cold air filled his lungs and chilled his bare skin. It made him feel awake and alive again, like he'd been asleep for days, which he more or less had been.

The droids in charge of garden maintenance had done their job and cleared the stone-paved area he'd claimed for his morning practice. He drained his mug, set it aside, and moved to the middle of the space.

The drills were as familiar to him as his own hands

—first the stretching and then a series of strikes, kicks, wing sweeps, and spins that refreshed his body and cleared his mind. He repeated the drills, speeding them up each time.

By the time he stopped, he felt like himself again, clear headed and ready for whatever challenges the day would bring. Oddly, he found himself wondering if one of those challenges would be Skye. He hadn't heard from her yet. Had her *mahoyen* finally found their wayward mate and claimed her? The thought of her with someone else didn't sit right. It settled in his chest, thick and heavy with emotions no spymaster should feel: anger and jealousy.

Distracted by his feelings, he didn't notice he wasn't alone until Skye spoke. "For someone who enjoys giving orders so much, you're not very good at following them. Aren't you supposed to be taking it easy?"

He spun around and spotted Skye leaning up against a tree about fifteen meters away. She wore a light jacket and heavy boots but otherwise seemed unaffected by the cold. "How long have you been there?"

"This close? Not long. I came out once I saw you were winding down." She tapped her temple. "Cyborg vision, remember? I can see a lot further than you can. And I have to admit, the view was impressive."

He folded his wings and walked the perimeter of

the cleared area to cool down. "You were spying on me?"

Skye snickered. "Nope. That's your job. I'm here because I have an invitation to your next appointment."

He walked over to where he'd left his mug and picked it up before answering. "I wasn't aware I had any appointments, never mind one that included you." It came out harsher than he'd intended. Skye's expression tightened and then fell into a carefully neutral mask. *Qarf.* Whatever her reasons, this female had cared for him while he was sick. She deserved better than that.

"My apologies. That was uncalled for," he said as he came to join her.

"Yeah, it was." Skye pushed off from the tree trunk with enough force to trigger a cascade of snow from the branches overhead. Both of them were caught beneath it, cursing and laughing.

Skye shook her head and shoulders, dusting herself off as she scrambled to get out from beneath the tree. "Oops."

Yardan followed and tried to ignore the trickles of cold water running down his body and into the waistband of his pants as the snow still stuck to him melted. He unfurled his wings and shook them to clear away more of the snow, gritting his teeth as water trickled over the highly sensitive spot at the base of his wings. An unexpected wave of arousal surged through him, strong enough he was tempted to shove his head in the nearest snowbank until he cooled off.

What in the name of the ancestors was wrong with him? Was this some odd side effect of his illness? It had to be. He glanced over at Skye. She was stunning, especially now with snow in her hair, her cheeks reddened by the cold, and the echoes of her laughter still in his ears.

And now he was waxing poetic. It was almost as if he was... Yardan stiffened. No. There's no way that could happen. This female was not his *mahaya*. He could not be experiencing the *sharhal*.

"This appointment. Since you're apparently more informed than I am, I'd like to know who we're supposed to meet."

"Rae made the appointment with your AI assistant. Didn't it inform you?"

"Rae?"

"The medical program with the snazzy hologram," Skye explained.

"Ah. And no, my AI didn't inform me. Then again, it's programmed not to disturb me until after my morning routine is complete."

Skye laughed softly. "Surprise. You have a meeting. It's in your office and it won't take long."

He shot her a suspicious glance. "You seem well-informed."

She smirked at him. "Oh, I am. For once, Spymaster, I know more than you do."

He didn't know which made him more uneasy... the fact she knew more than he did, or how gleeful she was about whatever he was about to learn.

He directed her to his office and then went to his rooms to clean up and change as quickly as possible.

"Computer, do I have a meeting this morning?"

"You have two."

"And you didn't inform me until now?" he grumbled as he dressed. "You've earned yourself a full reprogramming. Remind me to schedule that for later today. For now, who am I meeting with, when, and where?"

"Your first meeting is with the medical system and is due to start now. You have a meeting with Prince Tyran in half an hour."

"You are definitely getting reprogrammed. You can't tell me I'm due at a meeting after I'm already late."

He hurried back to his office, which wasn't far from his rooms. He heard two females conversing before the door opened, and he growled again at his AI's failure to alert him to this meeting. Not that it was entirely the program's fault. He had made it clear he wasn't to be disturbed until after his morning training. Computers were useful, but they had their limitations. That was why he preferred to handle most things himself.

He reached the door and paused long enough to school his features and square his shoulders. Only then did he enter his office to learn why the medical system wanted to speak with him—and why Skye had been invited to this meeting.

The cyborg in question stood erect but relaxed, her hands behind her back. She'd removed her coat, revealing a garment that was a blend of human and Vardarian fashion. It was sleeveless with a rounded collar and a simple pattern embroidered around it. The style and deep blue color complemented her appearance, but it was still strange to see the familiar design without the usual slits in the back to allow for wings.

She was conversing with the medical hologram, but both of them turned to face him as he walked to his desk.

"Good morning, Yardan," Rae nodded to him. "I understand there was a miscommunication with your AI assistant. I do apologize."

He waved off her apology and took a seat at his desk, gesturing for both females to sit despite the fact only one of them had a physical body. To his amusement, the hologram sat down but the cyborg didn't.

He quirked an eyebrow at Skye. "Is there a reason you wish to stay on your feet?" Normally that was a sign someone was expecting trouble.

Skye shrugged one shoulder. "I think it might be

best if one of us was standing for this conversation, and it shouldn't be you."

Well, that wasn't ominous. Nor was the glint of amusement in Skye's lovely eyes. Not at all. He nodded as if she'd commented on the weather instead of uttering a warning and nodded to Rae. "What is this meeting about, and why is Skye present for it?"

"Skye is present because this issue concerns you both." She smiled genially and then uttered a sentence he never expected to hear. "I ran tests on the samples you provided during your recovery. I have also done those same tests on Skye. Congratulations, Yardan. You are both experiencing the early stages of the *sharhal*. You are a match."

The cyborg was right. He needed to be sitting down right now.

"A match. How?"

"While some of what was done after you took your vows was medical, a portion of your nanotech was extracted, reprogrammed, and reintroduced into your body. The altered nanobots had the ability to suppress certain responses, along with the pheromones those responses would elicit. Given the unique circumstances of this mating, your symptoms are milder, for now."

He put the pieces together the moment Rae mentioned nanotech. Their enemy had recently exposed the colony to something that somehow deactivated the nanotech every Vardarian was born with. It was why they'd gotten sick in the first place. In his case, it had done more than make him vulnerable to illness and other physical insults. It had...

He looked at Skye. *Qarf.*

He'd expected her to tease him, or at the very least inform him that she'd told him so. She didn't say a word, though. She simply stood there, watching him, her expression fixed and neutral. Her eyes, though... they held a myriad of emotions, too many for him to read.

"You were right," he said.

Her lips rose for the briefest moment into a ghost of a smile. "So were you. This shouldn't have happened."

He caught it then. The note of uncertainty in her voice. Why was she off-balance, though? She'd been so cocky and confident just yesterday. The hologram glanced between them and then cleared her throat. It was an odd thing for a projection of light particles to do given she didn't have a throat or lungs, but it did pull their focus back to Rae.

"Do you have any further questions of me, Yardan?"

He had dozens, but none of them would change the facts. The hows and whys could wait. "Just one for the moment. Will the medical procedures done previously affect the *sharhal*?"

"I have reviewed all medical records and determined that this has never happened before, so I cannot be certain of anything. I believe that while it may alter your experience, it will not affect the final result. Skye is your *mahaya*."

"Thank you. That will be all." The hologram nodded to him and then to Skye before vanishing.

"You can say it," he said to Skye.

She lifted one blonde brow. "Say what?"

"That you told me so."

That smile reappeared, and this time, it lingered a little longer. "I did, but now I understand why you didn't believe me." She lifted one hand, turning it palm upward. "I know this isn't what you expected."

He barked out a rueful laugh. "The *sharhal* is never expected, Skye. That's part of the experience."

Her shoulders relaxed as she grinned, just a little. "It's a hell of a way to start a relationship. Surprise! You're mated... it's this or madness and death. Choose wisely."

Her comment reminded him that while he'd been unaware of the situation, she'd been experiencing the mating fever for several days already. That couldn't be pleasant for her. "You're not experiencing too much discomfort?"

Even as he said it, he realized just how stilted and awkward that sounded.

"It's nothing I can't handle for the moment. You have time to adjust and decide what you want to do."

"What I want to do? This is the *sharhal*. What choice do I have?"

Skye winced and he belatedly registered how that must sound to her. She wasn't Vardarian. She hadn't lived her life aware that one day she'd cross paths with her mates and that would be that.

Before he could correct course, Skye spoke up. "You *do* have a choice, though. You can have your nanotech altered and re-injected. As I understand the process, that should stop things. You don't have to do this."

"But that would leave you..."

Her expression was as fierce as any warrior. "I already told you. I'd rather go through hell again than take someone else's choice away from them. The choice is yours, Yardan. I've already made mine."

Brave, beautiful, and determined to do the right thing. He saw her so clearly, shining like the first star of evening. She was everything he could ask for in a mate, but to claim her, he'd have to turn his back on a lifetime of duty and sacrifice.

The ancestors were testing him... and he had no idea what the right answer was. All he knew was that no matter what he chose to do, it would come at a price he'd pay for the rest of his life.

6

"I ALREADY TOLD YOU. I'd rather go through hell again than take someone else's choice away from them. The choice is yours, Yardan. I've already made mine." Skye tried to read the spymaster's expression, but it was like trying to guess the emotions of a comet.

Everything about this male was impossible to intuit. Even his office was stripped down to the bare essentials, offering no hint of the being who spent his days here. Flat white walls, a black carpet, and stark furnishings that were purely functional without any personal touches. Not even a plant or a single artistic element was present.

She guessed he was surprised and possibly even angry right now. She could understand that. Unlike his brethren, he hadn't expected to find his mate. In fact, he'd made a deliberate choice to ensure he'd remain alone his entire life. What frustrated her was that she couldn't read any of that on his face, not even in the micro expressions most beings exhibited.

She couldn't help but wonder what crazy quirk of fate had linked their lives this way. He was a male who shunned emotions and had sacrificed everything for duty. She was a cyborg created to be a conflicted combination of soldier and caretaker. Still, she'd spoken the truth. She'd made her choice. Now their future was up to him.

Yardan lowered his head in a solemn gesture that was almost a bow. "Witnessed." Then he raised his gaze, and she found herself looking at the male behind the mask.

His smile was genuine, and for the first time she noticed he had a small dimple in one cheek, its presence almost hidden by his short beard. She'd spent hours at his bedside over the last few days, but he'd been asleep for most of it. She'd learned the shape of his face and body as she spent hours looking at the tattoo of some kind of a thorny vine that encircled his left biceps and wondering what it symbolized. Despite that, he seemed different now he was awake and well again.

"I suppose we should start getting to know each other." He offered her his hand, and she took it, surprised at the gesture. It was the first time they'd touched since he'd recovered, and she braced herself for another surge of lustful thoughts and desires—but instead of a tidal wave, it was more of a pond ripple, present but not overwhelming. The treatment Rae had provided was working. "I am Yardan. It is an honor to meet you."

"Hello, Yardan. I am Skye. The honor is mine, Spymaster." She released his hand and tipped her head to one side. "Do you have any other names? I don't, but I've noticed most Vardarians do."

"I relinquished my family name when I became *Naram T'kar*."

She took a moment to process his statement. He'd given up so much, even part of his name, to take on his current role. Then she'd come along and altered the trajectory of his life. "I never had a name before I got to Haven. I was just a number. You gave your name up to mark your transition to your new role. I claimed one for the same reasons."

"Why that name? Why Skye?" he asked.

It was easier to talk with him like this. They were having a conversation, not trading barbs or interrogating one another. "Because I'd never seen the sky before I woke up here in Haven. To me, it represented everything I'd never known—wide open spaces and freedom. To be honest, I'm envious of your species. Your wings let you go places I can't. At least, not without a shuttle."

"Have you ever been flying with one of us?" he asked, looking as surprised as she was at the question.

"Never. It seems..." she shrugged. "Intimate somehow."

"It can be. But it's also exhilarating." Yardan paused and then cleared his throat. "I have a meeting I need to attend and work to do but I would... I mean if you'd like, I could take you flying. Say, late this afternoon?"

"Are you asking me out on a date?"

"Vardarians don't date, but we do attempt to spend some time alone with our mates once we find them as part of the process of getting to know each other."

"That sounds a lot like a date to me. Are you going to bring flowers to this meeting, too?"

"Flowers would not fare well during a winter flight," Yardan pointed out.

"Good point. So maybe it's not a date. But yes, I'd like to go flying with you."

Her comm unit chirped, and she swore under her breath. "But for now, I need to get going. You're not the only one with another meeting on their agenda." She shook her head. "Of all the things I imagined a life of freedom would entail, I never factored how much of my time would be spent meeting with other beings, talking, and making plans."

Yardan threw back his head and laughed. The deep, booming notes were rich with amusement, hinting at sides of this male she hadn't suspected. "Life rarely brings us what we expect," he agreed once his laughter faded.

She snickered and pointed to herself and then at him. "You can say that again."

Before either of them could say anything else, a computerized voice interjected. "Forgive the intrusion, but if you do not depart soon, you will be late for your next meeting, Yardan."

The spymaster scowled in annoyance. "Yes, yes. I'm on my way. Don't get your coding in a twist."

The speed he transitioned back into his role as the thorny, cantankerous spymaster was startling, and it made the difference between the male she'd caught a glimpse of and the male standing here now even more obvious. How much of himself had Yardan sacrificed in the name of duty?

"Contact me when your work is finished," she said.

"My work is never finished." He looked almost apologetic for a moment. "Which is why those in my role are not supposed to have connections to others. It's difficult for everyone."

"I can see that." She could also see he was retreating again, settling in behind walls he'd built up over years, probably even decades.

He gave a sharp nod and gestured for her to take the lead as they both moved toward the door. "I will contact you, Skye. We do need time alone to talk."

"And fly." She winked at him over her shoulder. "Don't forget that part."

"I won't. In fact, I'm looking forward to it."

She heard something in his voice that hadn't been there before—something that sent a thrill of desire down her spine and made her breath catch in her throat. She snapped her gaze forward and made straight for the door. Phaedra had warned her about this. The more time she spent in Yardan's company, the more intense the mating fever would become. She'd hoped the treatment Rae had given her would have altered that, but apparently even Vardarian medicine had limits. It would be best if she spent some time away from him before their date. They had time. Not a lot of it, but hopefully it would be enough. Now she'd had a glimpse of his true self, she wanted him to say yes, not to save her life... but so she could save him from the lonely shadows where he seemed determined to live.

The problem was, she didn't know what part of her wanted that. Was it her heart, the *sharhal*, or her *fraxxing* programming? She needed time and space to figure that out. Maybe after her next meeting, she'd go for a long run in the woods.

Once they were in the corridor, she stopped and turned to stay goodbye to Yardan. "I will see you later, then. Try not to work too hard on your first day back. Send me a message so I know what time to meet you."

He shot her an amused look. "I am older than you by decades, female. Do not attempt to mother me. I have work to do and a spy to catch."

"You don't look that old. Maybe later you can tell me just how many decades you've been alive." Vardarian lifespans were long, but she couldn't imagine he was more than forty or fifty years old.

Maybe sixty at the top end. That would still make him decades older than she was, though. Like all cyborgs, she'd come out of her tank as a physically and mentally mature adult with programming and conditioning taking the place of life experience.

"Tonight we'll talk about all of that."

"Until tonight then." She held out her arm with her fingers curled into a loose fist. Yardan raised his, and they touched the backs of their wrists together. It was a Vardarian gesture she'd learned, but this time it felt different... intimate.

With their goodbyes said, she turned in the direction of her next meeting.

To her surprise, Yardan fell in beside her. They walked in silence for several paces before they exchanged looks of amused confusion.

"Who are you meeting with?"

"The prince. You?" he asked.

"I'm seeing the princess."

One corner of his mouth turned down, and then Yardan sighed. "Where is your meeting?"

She'd already come to the same conclusion he seemed to have drawn. With a wry laugh, she pointed down the hall toward the prince's meeting rooms. "I'll bet you drinks and a serving of N'tev's amazing new dessert that we're going to the same *fraxxing* place."

"I believe the human expression here is something like 'you're on.'"

She raised her brows. "You're taking that bet?"

"I am not. I know a trap when I see one." He shot her an unexpectedly wicked grin. "But I am curious to sample this dessert you mentioned. And Anya's place serves the best mochas on the planet."

"So the spymaster has a sweet tooth. Good to know."

He actually winked at her. "Don't go telling anyone my secrets, female."

Before she could answer, his demeanor changed back to that of the hard-edged and distrustful spymaster. Still, he'd given her another glimpse at the male beneath his mask... and she wanted to learn more about him. Apparently Phaedra felt the same way. Why else had she arranged things so they'd both be attending the same meeting?

Phaedra was up to something, and she'd dragged her *mahoyen* into her plans.

This would be an interesting meeting.

"Shall we go and see what our prince and princess wish to speak to us about?" she asked.

Yardan looked as disgruntled as a *gharshtu* that missed its dinner. "Let's."

They walked in together. As expected, Tyran and Phaedra were waiting for them.

Phaedra grinned like a Jeskyran who'd just won the jackpot. "You're here. And you came together. Perfect." She gestured for them both to sit before either of them could even acknowledge the prince.

"Sire?" Yardan asked.

"Sit, my friend. I hate to break this to you..." Tyran looked almost apologetic. "But my mate organized this meeting. I'm here to support her idea because I believe it's in the best interests of the colony."

"The *whole* colony," Phaedra added.

All the pieces fell into place, and Skye knew exactly what her friend was up to. She just didn't know if she wanted to hug the woman... or strangle her.

7

———

IT TOOK ALL his willpower not to stomp back to his office and lock the door behind him. If he did, he'd be able to work in peace, but only for as long as it took for the wily princess to come up with a new way to punish him.

She'd told him it was "... for the good of the colony that you learn to work with the other races, Yardan. We're all in this together."

He'd already admitted that issuing a decree ordering all non-Vardarians to stay in their homes and leave the care of the Vardarians to their own kind had been a mistake. He'd spent his career working for the former emperor and then the prince, surrounded by his own species as they bickered, postured, and backstabbed their way around the halls of power. Back there, his choice would have been the correct one. Here, though? He'd quickly seen his mistake. The other races—no, the other citizens of Haven—had come together to end the crisis.

His punishment was to work with Skye as a team to track down the spy still in their midst.

He didn't need a team. He was the prince's spymaster. This was his sworn duty. Skye didn't even have the correct training for this sort of work. But she was following him back to his office in silence. Was she happy about this? Angry? How could he work when the female he was supposed to be bonded to was in the same room as him?

She'd be a distraction, and he couldn't afford those right now. Not that Phaedra had listened to him when he'd made all these same arguments. She'd waved it off, and the prince had supported her.

That was another source of confusion. Phaedra was human. She likely didn't know the strict rules that governed his position, but Tyran did. Yet he hadn't said a word as Yardan had explained the situation with Skye, which wasn't easy when the cyborg was present and listening to every word.

Even more frustrating, Skye had let her expression turn as blank and impassive as stone. In fact, she'd moved so little it was like sitting next to a sculpture of a beautiful female instead of the real thing.

Tyran had simply listened to Yardan repeat all the rules and expectations of his position without comment. Once he'd finished reminding the prince of all the reasons he could not have a mate, Tyran had simply nodded and said, "I am aware of the rules and traditions of our homeworld, my friend. I am also aware we are not on the homeworld anymore. We came here to forge our own lives and make our own rules. I see no reason to keep the ones you just mentioned."

An AI chimed in mere seconds later, reminding the prince he had another meeting to attend. Yardan and Skye were back in the hallway less than a minute later, and Yardan suspected that everything he'd just experienced was a setup.

He'd just been played by his own protégé, or worse, by his protégé's mate.

"For the record, I didn't know anything about this," Skye said as they walked down the corridor.

He slowed his pace and twitched his fingers to gesture for her to catch up with him. "I'm certain you didn't. This is the princess's plan... and my punishment."

Skye hissed between her teeth. "I'm a punishment?"

Qarf. That came out wrong. What was it about this female that made his brain flap and flutter like a fledgling taking its first flight?

"Not you. This." They arrived at his office and he pointed to the door. "This is a... lesson. A reminder that I made the wrong decision during the crisis. "

"Being a lesson isn't any better than being a punishment." Skye folded her arms and turned to face him. "If you don't want this, say so. I'll talk to Phaedra and get her to see that what she's doing isn't helping our situation."

"Our situation?"

She huffed out a frustrated breath. "Yes. You and me. The sharhal. She knows, Yardan. And she's trying to help by putting us together. This isn't about what you did." She paused. "Okay, it's that, too, but that's not all she's trying to do here. She resisted the *sharhal* when it first took hold. She told me how difficult it was and how much it hurt her and her *mahoyen*. She's trying to help."

The female had attempted to achieve several goals with one action. Yardan was reluctantly impressed. "Are all humans as cunning as the princess?"

Skye uttered a wry laugh. "She's more gifted than some, but it would be wise not to underestimate them."

"Witnessed." He opened the door and gestured for her to enter first. He didn't ask his next question until the door closed behind them. "You said I shouldn't underestimate *them*. You don't see yourself as human?"

"I'm not human. Not entirely. I'm a mixture of human genetic material, bio-mechanical implants, and nanotech. Someone dumped all that into a maturation tank, stirred it together, and waited to see what popped out." Skye held out her arms, palms up. "Tada. Cyborg number 879A2QR7B, at your service."

"No." He spat the word like it was poison.

"No?" Skye lowered her hands and looked at him in bewilderment. "No what?"

"No, that's not who you are. Or all you are. Don't ever let me hear you describe yourself like that again." He heard the words coming out of his mouth, but he had no control over his mouth at this moment. His brain had been hijacked by something—the *sharhal*. By all the winds that blew, that had to be it.

"I..." Skye uttered that single syllable and then stopped talking again. Emotions chased across her face like clouds scuttering past the sun.

Silence hung between them for several seconds, and then she cracked a smile. "Wow. That was..."

"Out of line?"

Her smile widened. "For Yardan the spymaster, yes. But for Yardan my *mahoyen*, maybe not." She gave him an intent look. "You meant that. Didn't you?"

"Every word." He met her gaze. "I have many flaws, but I never lie to those who are close to me." It was one of the few rules he'd set for himself early in his training. He'd always had one being in his life he could be honest with about everything he chose to share.

Skye reached out to him, brushing her hand up his bare arm. "I get it now. That's why you don't let many close to you. Isn't it? You can't be honest with everyone or you couldn't do your job."

She understands. Not many did. His duty required that he stay in the shadows, listening to whispers and guarding against all manner of dangers. It was different here on Liberty. The colony was so young and fresh that intrigue and court politics were almost nonexistent. When Tyran's father sat on the throne, it had often seemed like the entire capital was embroiled in some plot or another. Talus's early and unexpected death had thrown everything into chaos with factions appearing overnight. Old grievances and new rivalries turned friends into enemies and enemies into corpses. Yardan had done all he could to relay information and advice to an unprepared princess rocked by grief. Only Neya hadn't wanted his council. In fact, she hadn't wanted him at all.

Tyran had come to him only hours after his rejection and offered him a place at his side. He'd agreed, thinking the prince would make a play for the throne. He had the support of the people and the military. His twin sister was ill-suited and unprepared for her new role. If Tyran had been born first...

But the prince didn't want his father's throne. He wanted to build something new, something better. Haven colony.

"You've gone quiet. Did I get it wrong? Is there some other reason you keep yourself so closely guarded?" Skye asked.

He'd been lost in thought, which never happened, at least not until he'd met Skye. "You aren't wrong. Your words made me reflect on matters I hadn't thought about for some time."

"Sorry about that. I spend most of my time

counseling others, and it's a hard habit to break. Especially since, well—" She gestured vaguely to the side of her head. "Default programming. You know."

He didn't know what she was referring to, and that bothered him almost as much as the fact she thought he already had the information she referred to. He wanted to ask for more information, but decided they had bigger issues to deal with first.

"We are all a product of our training." He tapped his chest. "As you've already noted."

That made her chuckle. "Yeah." She looked around his office appraisingly. "Where would you like me?"

The first thing that flashed through his mind was a vivid image of Skye bent over his desk as he... *Qarf.* No. That was not happening. He had a job to do, and it didn't involve nudity, pleasure, or anything else the *sharhal* was actively enticing him to do with, and to, Skye.

He locked down his libido, but he wasn't fast enough. Skye reacted to his arousal, releasing her own pheromones in response to his. Her cheeks flushed with color and her lips parted slightly, as if in anticipation.

They both froze for a second. If she moved toward him, would he have the strength to turn away? He wasn't sure. He wasn't even sure he wanted to try.

This was why all *Naram T'kar* foreswore close connections and the possibility of finding their mate. It was all so damned distracting.

"Whoa." Skye took two steps backward and shook her head. "I'm going to need my own office. There's no way we're getting anything done if we're in the same room."

She looked over at his desk and then back to him, and he swore the color in her cheeks intensified. "At least not anything productive."

Had she read his mind? Some of the cyborgs had empathic abilities, but Skye's name hadn't been listed as one of them. No, she hadn't done that... they'd just been of the same mind because of the *fraxxing* mating fever.

"You're right. I'll arrange for a room across the hall. Will that suit?"

"That will be fine. Just have your AI update me about what you're working on over here, so we're not covering the same ground."

Yardan nodded. "It will take a few minutes for the staff to get everything set up. That office has never been used." He moved around his desk and took his seat before nodding for her to do the same. "Until then, let me catch you up on what we know and what we don't." Not that he intended to tell her everything. Not yet. *Sharhal* or not, she was still a suspect, and so were many of her friends.

He had to stifle a laugh when Skye grabbed the back of a chair and carried it to the corner that put the most space between them. She set it down backward and then straddled it so her arms crossed over the back.

She looked like a predator waiting to pounce—sensual, powerful, and in control.

His cock was hard enough to drill through hull plating right now, and all they'd done was talk. If it was this bad for him with all his senses dulled, what must she be going through right now?

They needed to focus.

"Computer. New task list in order of priority. One, increase air circulation in my office to maximum. Two, contact D'kor and inform him that the office across from mine needs to be made ready as soon as possible for Skye. See to it she has all the necessary codes and clearances. Three, have two mochas delivered to this office as soon as possible."

"It will be done," the computer responded.

"Mochas again?" Skye asked.

"When I find something I like, I stick with it. The princess thinks that makes me boring."

Skye waved her hand. "Phaedra thinks most things are boring. I'm more interested in what *you* think? Does consistency make you uninteresting and dull?"

He barked out an unintended laugh. "Some days, yes. Others?" He shrugged and gave her the unvarnished truth. "Some days it all goes nova and I'm caught in a whirlwind of lies, treachery, and danger. Those days remind me how important it is to enjoy the simple things."

"Like mochas and working out in the snowy silence of morning?"

Veth, she had a gift for understanding others... Maybe she'd be useful to him as more than just a source of information about the non-Vardarian colonists.

Not that he'd admit it to her or to the interfering, pink-haired princess who had insisted they work together "for the good of the colony."

Females were a pain in the ass. Which is why he had avoided them as much as possible... until now.

8

———

Skye walked into her new office and closed the door. She didn't drop her guard until the chime confirmed she was out of sight and hearing of anyone else. Then she sighed in relief and slumped against the wall beside the doorway.

The medical treatment Rae had given her helped to minimize her reaction to Yardan, but it didn't shut it down completely. She was still distracted and aroused when she was in his company, which meant she had to fight to stay focused while her libido smoldered and sparked.

Since a cold shower wasn't on the agenda, she opened every window in her new office and then stood in the draft, letting the winter air cool her off. The sun bounced off the snow-covered garden outside, filling her vision with dazzling stretches of white. The stark view helped clear her mind almost as much as the fresh air, and before long, she closed the windows.

It was time to get to work.

She settled into the chair behind her desk, leaned back, thought about the briefing she'd just had. It had been thorough, but something told her the spymaster hadn't told her everything. *Stubborn bastard.* She'd be more help if he wasn't keeping secrets.

Yardan was bull headed, resistant to change, and thornier than a Jeskyran's ball sack. But based on the briefing he'd just given her, Skye had to admit he was good at his job. No, not just good. He excelled at it. He was tactical, organized, and incredibly well-informed, especially given he'd been ill for the last few days.

She had expanded his intelligence based on the data files the cyborgs had shared with each other over the course of the crisis. Organic memories were flawed and incomplete, but cyborgs could capture moments with perfect recall and extensive detail. It gave the spymaster a chance to review data from various times and locations, and unlike her partner, she handed over everything she had without reservation.

"You all have this ability?" he'd asked as he scrolled through the new information.

"We do. We can capture data and share it in real time or save it for future review."

He scowled and tapped his chin. "I wasn't informed about this."

Again with the paranoia? Skye had scowled back at

him despite the fact he hadn't looked up from his reading. "Yes, you were. I saw the report. Hell, I helped write parts of it. We haven't hidden anything from you." She sneered, letting her mood leak into her next words. "If we had, you'd have discovered it and had us thrown back into our cryopods."

She folded her arms and glared. "I know what your duty requires, Yardan. You were protecting the colony. At least, the parts of it you recognized at the time. We're all aware that you weren't happy that Haven's population included cyborgs."

"I wasn't," he admitted. "But given what I was told, I had reason to be concerned." The corner of his mouth twitched upward. "At that time."

"And now?" She wasn't ready to let this go.

Yardan lifted one shoulder in the Vardarian version of a shrug. "You and your brethren took care of us when we couldn't care for ourselves. So did the humans."

"And?" she prompted him.

He gave her a grudging nod. "Times have changed. The cyborgs have proven to be loyal citizens and friends."

She noted he hadn't mentioned the human colonists, but that was a battle for another day. After all, one of the humans *had* released the nano-swarm that wiped out the Vardarians' nanotech. Kara had fooled everyone, including her.

Kara. Skye cursed in three languages, paused, and

then added another in Jeskyran just for good measure. Kara had betrayed the entire colony and put countless lives at risk, all in the name of greed and xenophobia. Haven wasn't supposed to be like that. This place was intended to be better. A community built on trust and acceptance.

Yardan had raised both brows at her outburst.

She'd waved a hand and sighed before explaining. "Sorry, that wasn't about you. I was thinking about Kara. She betrayed us all. The colonists are good souls, and Kara's actions stained them all and made it look like the first batch of humans that showed up included at least one intent on ruining everything."

"Indeed it does." He nodded once. "And betrayal always hurts. Trust is a delicate thing. Once it's broken..." He trailed off.

"Yeah. Now we're left to pick up the pieces and try to make sure that's the last time it happens." She'd left shortly afterward, and her last words had followed her back to her office.

The easiest way to protect Haven is to stop bringing in outsiders. The moment the thought popped into her head, she shoved it out again. That wasn't a kind thought or a fair one. She knew that, but despite what she'd told Yardan about being a cyborg, Skye also knew she was all too human, with the same flaws and potential for darkness as any of them. Only she was faster, stronger, and more dangerous than any human could ever be. Which was why the rest of the galaxy had been more than happy to sign the agreement that sent Skye and the rest of the survivors of Reamus Research Station to Haven Colony, so long as none of them ever tried to leave.

Haven was their home, and someone wanted to destroy what they were building here. The question was, who the *fraxx* was it?

It didn't take her long to copy over Yardan's working files and add her own information to the growing collection of data. Once she had it all, she reorganized it to suit her needs and capabilities. Unlike Yardan, her ability to recall data was perfect. She could also scan and upload portions of the reports almost instantaneously.

It was part of her design, but she didn't often get a chance to utilize it. In fact, the last time she'd done anything like this she'd been working on her qualifications to become a counselor. It had sped up some elements of her training, but not all of it. Some things had to be learned by doing them. She could retain and review every scrap of data Yardan had access to, but she'd still need to find the thread that wove this conspiracy together.

Conspiracy. That was an interesting choice of words. Was her subconscious trying to tell her something?

Skye looked around the small office she'd claimed for herself. Holo-projections covered the walls, and she'd designated part of the ceiling as a rogues' gallery of possible suspects. So far, the only face up there was Kara's.

Another list sat behind her desk, this one minimized to barely half a meter across. On it were the names of the colonists she could be certain were not involved. It already included her own name, the princess and her consorts, most of the leadership council, and various humans and cyborgs. It was a relatively short list, but it would get longer soon. Yardan's current focus was to work out how their spy contacted her handler. Her task was to cull their list of suspects down to something more manageable. Then they'd cross-reference their findings and look for matches.

This would take a while.

The list had grown by more than a thousand names by the time she stopped for the day. She'd started with the obvious choices—children. While they might be susceptible to trickery, recruiting would be difficult. All the children at the colony were Vardarians and had come here directly from their former homes with their families.

While it was possible some kids could have been approached over the datasphere, it wasn't likely. Security kept a close watch for nonstandard and suspicious communication traffic, which meant initial contact would be difficult. Besides, the enemy was after intel. She couldn't see them relying on a child to see the big picture or know what to look for and report.

Her door chimed, announcing a visitor.

"Cat, activate open door protocol."

"Of course, Skye."

"Thank you." The door opened before she finished speaking while all the projections went blank.

Yardan stepped inside and nodded in approval as he saw all the empty space. He hadn't mentioned anything about securing their investigation, but it was obvious they couldn't risk anyone seeing what they were doing.

"I thought I'd come over and see how you're doing with your side of things."

"Progressing." She suspected he was here to see what she was up to and whether she was doing it to his standards. *Males.* "You?"

"Progressing," he replied.

The door closed, and she gestured for him to take a seat. "You going to elaborate?"

"Not yet. You?"

She crossed her arms over her chest. "Are we really doing this? It's only the first day and you're already trying to stonewall me."

He shook his head. "That's not it. I'm not used to..." he tapped his chest, his fingers striking the ornate collar of his top just above where it split to reveal golden skin over hard muscle. "This. Sharing intel.

Especially when I don't have anything solid yet. I've got nothing but guesswork and theories spinning around like dust motes in a whirlwind. It's too soon to commit to anything."

Her mouth engaged before her brain could hit the brakes. "Did you just say you don't do commitment?"

She expected him to either ignore her jibe or toss one back at her. Instead, he arched one brow and gave her a look that sent frissons of desire down her spine and made heat pool deep in her core. "I don't commit to anything until I'm certain it's the right choice. Rushing in leads to unmet expectations, and I have no intention of *disappointing* anyone. First rule of investigation is to do your research and make sure you know how to proceed. Only then do you make your move."

"Uh. Right. No sense um, rushing to failure. Right?" Her voice sounded high and breathless, even to her. What in the name of gravity did he just say? Was he talking about the investigation or something *else*?

Her brain wasn't sure, but her body was stuffing the ballot box in favor of the second option. Would he bring that same intensity and focus into the bedroom? The idea gave her goosebumps.

"I don't rush anything."

Veth, was she imagining it, or had he stressed that last word? What was happening here? Was he flirting, or was the *sharhal* making her imagine things?

"I'll uh... take that under advisement."

"Good." He nodded toward one of the windows. "The sun will set soon. If you wish to fly with me, we should get going."

She took a moment to switch gears and catch up with his current topic. "Flying. Right. I'd love it. If you're done for the day, so am I."

He chuckled and actually cracked a smile, which softened his features and made him look even more handsome... *dammit.* "I'll be back at it tonight, but even I take breaks once in a while."

"I'll believe that when I see it for myself." She rose and walked around her desk to join him. "Shall we?"

"You'll need something warmer."

"No I won't. All cyborgs come with environmental controls. My medi-bots will keep me from freezing."

His dark brows furrowed. "That's not the same as keeping you warm. I have nanotech too, and I still prefer to wear a cloak or jacket when I fly in the winter."

"I'll be fine. I was created to survive and function in extreme environments." She didn't know why she was working so hard to remind him she was made in a lab instead of born. Maybe because she needed him to see her for who and what she was. If this had any chance of working, they'd both have to embrace an uncomfortable level of honesty.

"Are all cyborgs as stubborn as you?" he asked.

She flashed him a smile as she walked past him to the door. "It's a flaw the Grays and their minions never managed to eradicate." Her tone was light, but a dark truth lurked beneath her words. The Gray Men had tested, tortured, and twisted their creations in unimaginable ways as they attempted to create the perfect cybernetic warrior—a killing machine with no empathy, no sense of self, and no soul.

His hand landed on her shoulder, drawing her up short. "I'm glad."

She turned back to look at him. "Glad that I'm stubborn?"

Yardan grinned, his white teeth showing beneath his dark beard. "At least you're not afraid to speak your mind."

He squeezed her shoulder lightly. "I meant I'm glad they didn't break you, Skye. The universe would be a less interesting place without you."

Their eyes met, and before she knew what was happening, Yardan's hand moved, caressing her gently as he slipped his fingers up the side of her neck and into her hair. It took almost no pressure to draw her closer until barely a breath remained between his mouth and hers.

Anticipation sizzled in her veins, and she felt like she was drowning in the details of the moment. His green eyes gleamed like pale jade, illuminated by fire. The wood smoke and citrus scent of his skin filled her lungs. His skin gleamed like newly minted gold, his scales tightening as arousal claimed him.

"Skye," he whispered her name like a prayer, and then his mouth slanted across hers.

Heat tore through her as a hunger like nothing she'd ever experienced battered at her senses. He was all she could feel, taste, and touch, and she still couldn't get enough of him. His fingers tightened in her hair as he took control, his free arm locking around her waist to pull her in hard against his chest.

As tall as she was, she still had to rise on her toes to kiss him back. She caught hold of his collar in one hand to steady herself as she spread the fingers of her other hand across the hard planes of his chest. She'd been kissed before, but none of those males had been Yardan, and none of them made her feel like she was standing in the heart of a star, surrounded by flames yet completely safe.

The thought made her laugh, the sound bubbling up from her throat to spill into the heat of his mouth. Nothing was safe about any of this—but the *sharhal* didn't care about any of that, and right now, neither did she. She'd worry about everything else after he stopped kissing her like she was the last female in the universe.

Even as she thought it, part of her hoped that day never came. So of course, it ended the moment she made her wish.

9

———

CONTROL. Where the *qarf* was his control? He hadn't acted like this since he was a randy, moon-eyed youth chasing his first female. It was embarrassing. At least it would have been if Skye hadn't kissed him back. Thank the ancestors. She accepted his overture with an eagerness that poured rocket fuel on the flames already burning in his veins.

Her kisses were intoxicating, her lips warm and soft against his. His scales tightened everywhere she touched him, sending ripples of sensation across his body and arousing needs he'd refused to acknowledge for years beyond count. He'd opened a door he'd never intended to visit again, and he wasn't sure he could close it... or if he even wanted to try.

Now he'd gotten a taste of this beautiful female he didn't want to end this moment, but he had to. If this was truly happening—and part of him still clung to the hope that it was all a mistake—they needed more time. Not that the universe or his ancestors would give them much, but he had to try. He wanted time to get to know Skye, and he needed to give her the opportunity to learn at least a little about who he was. Even if opening himself up to another being was the last thing he ever expected to do.

Yardan lifted his head, willed his cock to soften, and sealed his lips against the groan of protest that rose in his throat.

He was in control, dammit. And he intended to stay that way.

Skye uttered a soft sigh as she stepped away from him. Her lips were swollen from his kisses as her hair fell around her face in disarray. She kept her hands on him as long as she could, and when she pulled away, he felt the loss of her touch like a chill wind blowing across his skin.

"That was unexpected," she said.

He found himself grinning. "Everything about this situation fits that description."

Her smile lit up her face and warmed the darkest parts of his soul. "True." She lowered her voice to a sultry whisper. "But I think I could get used to the unexpected."

It took all his considerable willpower not to haul her back into his arms again. By all the winds that blew, they were both in trouble.

He fisted his hands at his sides and blew out a

sharp breath. "I promised to take you flying. So that's what we're going to do."

"Right. Flying. That was the plan. We should do that. You. Me. Cold air. Good idea."

Cold air sounded like a very good idea right now. "I'll meet you in the hallway in two minutes. I just need to lock up."

"I'll be waiting." Her voice had a breathless quality that turned his cock to steel again in a heartbeat.

He nodded and left before she noticed the state he was in. He made it back to his office and made sure the door was closed before he slid a hand down his pants and rearranged his equipment to a less uncomfortable position.

"Get yourself together, old man. You're embarrassing yourself."

He strode over to an unmarked doorway that led to a small bathroom. He splashed a handful of cold water onto his face, blotted it with a towel, and then popped a breath freshening tab into his mouth without letting himself think too much about why he'd done that. He knew why. Because if he had Skye back in his arms again, he'd have no choice but to kiss her.

"Computer, log me as being out for dinner for the next two hours.

Secure all files and continue background searches while I'm gone."

"Order confirmed."

He took a few seconds to open a closet behind his

desk and retrieved his favorite winter garb from the assortment of garments inside. He kept an array of outfits in his office so he could change into whatever might be required without the need to return to his quarters when the unexpected happened.

He settled the fur-lined cloak over his shoulders, fastened it in place, and then arranged it so his wings could extend through the slits at the back. It was made to be worn in the air with enough weight to stop it from flaring out in the wind and throwing the wearer off balance. Nanotech or not, he liked to be comfortable whenever he could.

Skye waited for him in the hallway. She'd tied her hair back into a ponytail and donned the same light jacket she'd had on when he'd first seen her this morning. The dark blue color suited her, but part of him grumbled that it hid too much of her from view.

He preferred her to show a little skin... or a lot of it. If this was some kind of test, he was failing it. *Badly*.

They walked out into the winter twilight together, neither of them speaking. It was a comfortable silence, though, the kind he rarely got to enjoy. The chill air turned his breath to vapor, and the snow crunched beneath their boots as they returned to the spot where she'd found him that morning.

The brisk cold filled his lungs and cleared his head, rejuvenating him in ways he hadn't expected. Normally, he'd still be working at this time of day, eating his dinner at his desk and barely sparing a glance outside his window. He exercised each morning, but maybe something was to be said for taking a break before the evening meal. He hadn't even gone flying since he'd been cleared to go back to work. Now, anticipation had his wings twitching. It had been too long.

"How do we do this?" Skye asked once they'd reached the center of the cleared area. She gestured to herself and then to him. "I mean, do I just hold on, or is there a harness?"

"No harness. I'll carry you." He held out his arms as if holding her across his chest. "One arm around my neck will keep you balanced, but if you choke me, we're both going to land face first in a snowbank."

"No choking. Check." She moved closer to him, paused for an instant, and then closed the distance so she stood directly in front of him with her hand on his shoulder. "Like this?"

"Like this." He acted on impulse, wrapping her in the folds of his cloak before sweeping her off her feet and into his arms.

"I can't decide if you're being gallant or annoying," Skye said. Her words were light with barely concealed laughter.

"Probably both." He ignored the notes of desire

that deepened his tone and added a gravel-like edge to his voice. "Hold on."

Skye wrapped her arm around the back of his neck. "Ready."

He launched himself skyward, carrying them both into the purple-hued shadows of dusk.

It took several powerful beats of his wings to lift them into the air, and he had to circle the garden several times before they gained enough altitude to fly over the palace wall.

Skye whooped with joy as the lights of the colony came into sight. By the time night finished falling, the windows and doorways of Haven would automatically darken to protect against light pollution, but for now, the colony was awash in warm light.

The river that divided the colony was a crystalline serpent winding past Haven on its journey to the ocean. It was too dark to make out the coastline, leaving the line between land and sea lost to shadow.

He climbed until the last rays of the local star reappeared beyond the peaks of nearby mountains. It was a private sunset only the two of them witnessed, the clouds painted in shades of crimson, gold, and pink beyond the snow-covered mountaintops.

Skye moved in his arms, leaning in until her mouth was next to his ear. "It's beautiful!"

It was indeed. The fleeting glimpse of glory reminded him how fragile this new colony was and how quickly it could be consumed the same way the darkening night would soon devour this sunset. Soon nothing would be left of this moment but his memories. Then it struck him that he wasn't the only one bearing witness to this beautiful moment. Skye was here too. After a lifetime of experiencing so many moments alone, it was surprisingly good to share this one with her.

He flew them toward the mountains, chasing the sun until it vanished beneath the horizon. The sky darkened enough for the stars to appear, lighting the world beneath them with a cold glow that made him shiver despite his cloak.

This was his time—the time of shadows. He stole a glance at Skye and couldn't help but think that with her sunshine-colored hair and eyes as blue as a summer sky, she was meant to walk in the light of day. Why had the ancestors done this to him? To *them*. Because as strange as it was to imagine himself with a mate, at least Skye would bring some light into his world. All he could offer her was darkness and distrust.

He flew through the night, enjoying it more than he had in recent memory. In fact, he couldn't recall the last time he'd gone flying purely for the joy of it with no destination in mind and no reason to hurry.

Skye pointed out landmarks as they sped by, managing to convey her enthusiasm with a few shouted words and gestures. She knew more places than he did, a fact that made him realize he'd been spending too much time in his office and not enough exploring the colony. Even now, in the darkest stretch of winter, Haven continued to grow.

It annoyed him that they couldn't talk as they flew. He'd never been airborne with anyone he couldn't speak with through the implanted devices all Vardarians carried. Skye and the other cyborgs used different technology to communicate, tech he'd never been interested in—until now.

They were working together, after all. It would be smart for them to be linked so they could talk privately, no matter what situation they found themselves in. It was the practical thing to do.

And if he kept telling himself that, he might even start to believe it.

They flew over parts of the colony that had been nothing more than blueprints the last time he'd checked. Even the livestock pens had been expanded. He could see herds of the local herbivores called *noats* bedded down beneath open-walled shelters while flocks of the dangerous but delicious *gharshtu* filled the pens that encircled the *noats*. Probably using the *gharshtu* to protect the smaller animals from the predations of ghost cats and a nasty creature they'd recently discovered. The *kopaki* had large, powerful claws that allowed it to burrow through almost any terrain and tear about its prey with disturbing ease. The opportunistic hunters liked to ambush their intended meals from beneath the ground, and the *noat* pens had attracted their attention.

The *gharshtu* had taken an instant dislike to the smelly, fur-covered beasts and were quite happy to hunt any of the creatures that came into their pens.

An updraft created by the body heat of so many creatures allowed him to spread his wings and soar upward again, taking them so high the air dropped to well below freezing and the wind made his eyes tear.

Skye laughed and pointed toward the bridge that spanned the river. "Show me what you got, Spymaster!"

Feeling young, reckless, and only a little foolish, Yardan folded his wings and sent them into a power dive. The wind buffeted them as they sped headlong toward the bridge. Skye's enthusiastic hoots and calls barely reaching his ears before they were carried away by the rushing wind.

Pride puffed out his chest and made him grin when he pulled off a perfect landing. He touched down and then bent one knee, lowering himself just enough to allow Skye to regain her feet and move away.

Only she didn't.

Instead, she threw herself back into his arms, beaming and laughing. Her hair had torn free of its ponytail and fell around her face in disarrayed splendor and tears streamed across her windburned cheeks as she smiled up at him.

"Thank you! That was even better than I had imagined." Then, before he could answer, she kissed him. It was a fleeting touch of her lips to his, a flash of heat, a whispered promise of passion, and then she moved away as if it had never happened.

He wanted to reach for her, to pull her back into his arms and taste her lips again, but he didn't. He knew why she'd pulled away from him. They weren't alone. He flipped up the hood of his cloak to hide his face and then fell in beside Skye as they walked to the welcoming light and noise of the Bar None.

"Thank you," he said, his voice pitched low.

Skye turned and gave him a knowing smile. "I figured it might be a little soon for you to be ready to go public with all this." She paused and her smile widened. "Your reputation as the scary spymaster of Haven might never recover."

He scowled at her. "I'm not scary." Then he growled and raised his lips into a snarl. "I'm terrifying."

Skye laughed and bumped his shoulder with hers. "Holy *fraxx*. You have a sense of humor!"

"Shhh, don't tell anyone. It's a carefully guarded secret." He barely recognized himself at the moment. He had no friends he could be this relaxed around except the prince and his consorts, and while Tyran might be his friend, he was also his liege and master. Tradition and protocol dictated the limits of their relationship, now and always.

"Can we go flying again soon?" Skye asked.

He only had one answer to that question. "Yes, of course."

She brushed her hand over his. "Thank you."

That moment of contact sparked another blaze of need, this one short-circuiting his filters and common sense.

"The pleasure is mine, but before I take you flying with me, we need to make another sort of flight." He pointed upward. "You and I are going to the main orbital platform tomorrow morning."

She cocked her head. "*We* are?"

That hadn't been his intention. He'd planned on going alone and leaving Skye to continue her work here in Haven, but he couldn't take it back now without looking like a total *bakaffa*. At least that's what he told himself. The truth was, he wanted her company, and he'd take it any way he could.

That realization struck with the force of a rogue comet. He *wanted* Skye. There was no point in pretending this wasn't the sharhal anymore. It had to be. What he still didn't know was why the ancestors had done this to him or what would happen next.

10

It was cold, bleak, and blustery outside, but Skye barely noticed. Minor details like the weather didn't register because she had better things to think about—like her evening with Yardan.

Flying with him had been exhilarating, but the moments she valued the most were the ones they'd spent enjoying drinks and dessert while they got to know each other better. She'd told him about her first days in Haven and how wondrous she'd found even the most ordinary things—the sky, the weather, the scent of spring flowers on a warm breeze. She'd been created after the Resource Wars and, until her rescue, had never left the station where she'd been designed. She'd been one of the first cyborgs to wake up once they arrived at the colony, and she enjoyed telling him about the challenges and joys of helping first her fellow cyborgs and later the human colonists learn about this place and the beings that lived there.

In turn, Yardan had shared a bit of himself with her like stories of his childhood on the Vardarian homeworld and adventures shared with his cousins and companions. He laughed and joked, relaxing enough to let her see the male behind the mask he wore most of the time. Each time someone got too near them, the spymaster returned and his smile would fade away, only to re-emerge once they were alone again.

His body language changed, too. He would close himself off, his handsome face turning stony and his eyes cooling to a glacial green. Soon the surrounding tables had emptied, leaving them alone in one corner of the otherwise bustling tavern.

It was a good act, but that's all it was—an act. He adopted the persona and wore so often it had taken over as his default personality. But that wasn't who he was. She'd seen the real Yardan. He had a dimple in his cheek, a laugh like warm firelight, and a hard body she'd dreamed about more than once since he'd kissed her goodnight.

She'd dreamed about his kisses, too. Hard. Hungry. Demanding. In her fantasies, she'd given in to those demands and let him take whatever he wanted. She'd never desired that before. On Reamus, her programming wouldn't let her refuse any command she was given. She'd been used in every way imaginable, and once she was free, she'd sworn she'd never submit to anyone ever again.

She'd chosen only Vardarian lovers since coming to Haven. Their entire species enjoyed sex in all forms, but it was purely for enjoyment since every single Vardarian male dreamed of finding their *mahaya*, and no mated male had any interest in being with anyone besides their mate. That made them the perfect, no-strings-attached partners. But those days were behind her now. She'd found her mate, even if he came with a multitude of strings—most of them tied up in knots.

Yardan had sent her instructions detailing when and where to meet him. The message was sent while she slept, or tried to. Clearly, Yardan had stayed up late. She wondered if his work ethic or the mating fever had kept him awake. She hoped it was the latter. Knowing Yardan, it was probably a little of both.

His message had been brisk and businesslike, which she took as a sign that while they were on the proverbial clock, he intended to keep things professional and proper. In other words, he'd be in full spymaster mode, all growl, scowl, and business.

She understood he wasn't ready for more than that. Not when he was working, at least, which was fair enough. The *sharhal* had been a shock for both of them, but she'd had longer to adjust to the idea. She'd also been aware that finding a mate among the Vardarians could happen at any time. She'd been prepared for it, as much as one could, at least.

Yardan's experience was the opposite. He'd expected to go through his life alone, and then she'd arrived and turned his world upside-down.

This was why she'd taken the treatment to slow down the mating fever. He needed more time. If it weren't for Rae's assistance, the symptoms of the *sharhal* would already be difficult to endure. It was one of the reasons she'd chosen to walk to the spaceport. The cold air helped to clear her head.

Even now, just thinking about Yardan made her pulse pound and triggered a flood of liquid heat that pooled low in her belly.

When she arrived at the landing pad, she was surprised to discover their ride wasn't the prince's private shuttle. She'd assumed that's what they'd be taking because very little passenger traffic was coming and going from the orbital station. Most of what was transferred back and forth was freight being shuttled down from the ships too large to bring into Liberty's gravity well. The cargo shuttle waiting on the pad was a workhorse model designed for efficiency not comfort.

Yardan arrived less than a minute later. He flew straight in, following the carefully marked pathway that kept anyone not inside a ship from being struck or reduced to ash as they navigated the busy spaceport by land or air.

Even from a distance, he was instantly recognizable. He flew with the same precise control as he did everything else: efficient, powerful, and highly focused.

He landed about ten meters away, his legs moving the moment his feet touched the ground. His wings folded away as he walked, vanishing beneath his coat.

He wore a variation of the outfit she'd seen him in yesterday, which amounted to a whole lot of black—black boots, black pants, and a black vest. The vest had the usual rounded collar, though she noted this one had more ornate needlework than usual with gold and gemstones incorporated into the design. Over all this, he wore a long black coat that fell past his knees. It reminded her of the cloak he'd worn yesterday, though this material was lighter and the entire look was more tailored.

Unlike yesterday, he left his arms bare, showing off an impressive amount of muscle beneath his golden skin. It also showed the tattoo that circled one of his biceps. Her first inclination was to trace the lines with her fingers. Her second was to ask him why he had it. She'd done some reading, but so far she hadn't found anything to explain it.

He greeted her with a brief smile. "Good morning, Skye."

"Good morning. I hope you slept well."

A wry smile tugged at the corner of his lips, just enough to show her a flash of his dimple. "Not as well as I expected to."

"I'm sorry to hear that. It must be something in the air. I didn't sleep well either."

They exchanged a look hot enough to start the engines of every ship in the area, but before they could say anything else, their pilot arrived. The moment they were no longer alone, Yardan fell back into his brusque, businesslike manner, all flirtation gone.

The pilot turned out to be someone she knew, a cyborg named Thrash. He'd struggled to adjust to his new life on Liberty. After a lifetime of nothing but violence and suffering, colony life had been something of a shock. Skye was one of a team of counselors who worked with Thrash and the others to help them adapt, all while trying to come to terms with their new reality themselves.

"Hey, Thrash. How are things?" she greeted him.

"Things are good." He started to grin but then spotted Yardan and immediately blanked his expression. His next words came out with a crisp, almost military edge. "Spymaster Yardan. I understand I'll be taking you to the plat today."

Skye blinked. *Who are you and what have you done with the real Thrash?* She sent through the internal channels that linked every cyborg in the colony to each other.

Ha-ha. Funny. Do you know who that is?

I'm working with him, so yeah, I know. What's the issue?

You're working with him? My condolences. I

mean. I hear he's a serious hard case, and those are Edge's words, not mine. Who did you piss off to get assigned duty with the paranoid xenophobe?"

Fraxx. Was that what Edge was saying about the prince's advisor? She'd have to talk to him about that. There was enough tension between the various groups that made up the colony without throwing rocket fuel on that fire. Not to mention Edge was just as paranoid and distrustful of strangers as the spymaster.

"The plat?" Yardan asked.

Thrash shrugged. "That's what most of us call the orbital platform. I'm sure the leadership council will get around to giving it a proper name eventually, but for now, it's just the plat."

Yardan nodded. "I see. And yes, we're headed there to make some inquiries. When do we leave, Thrash? From what I've read, you are a precise pilot who keeps a tight schedule. I'd hate to negatively impact your performance record."

Skye caught Thrash's flicker of surprise when Yardan used his name, but he recovered so quickly she wasn't sure the spymaster noticed.

"We'll take off as soon as I confirm our cargo is loaded and you're both in your seats. Should be a quick flight, less than an hour."

Skye barely registered Thrash's answer. She was focused on what Yardan had done. Was he really trying to play power games with their pilot? Once they were alone, she intended to ask him about it. Someone had once told her about an old Earth expression concerning honey, flies, and vinegar. She had no idea why anyone would want to attract flying insects, but the adage had a good point, one that Yardan clearly didn't grasp. Maybe this was part of the reason fate had brought them together. She was the honey to his vinegar.

The thought made her snigger, but she managed to turn it into a light cough as she pointed to their ship. "Shall we get ourselves on board and buckled in? I haven't been off the planet since I got here. I'm looking forward to seeing it from orbit. I've heard it's really pretty from up there."

"It is," Thrash said. "Follow me. I'll show you to your seats. Apologies in advance, it's not really set up for passengers, especially not ones of your uh, distinction, Spymaster."

"We'll make do."

"It'll be fine," Skye chimed in. "I mean, the last time I was on a ship, I was in a cryo-pod flying as cargo. This has got to be an improvement."

Once they were seated and Thrash had left to check the load one last time, she wriggled in her seat and tried to find a position that didn't make her feel like an origami flower. "Okay, maybe traveling as cargo would be better."

Yardan quirked up one brow and then looked pointedly around the cramped space they were wedged into. "There is no *maybe* about it."

The passenger area was little more than an empty booth-sized section between the bulkhead of the freight area and the cockpit ahead of them. From the looks of it, this space had been an airlock at some point. Now it was an airlock-sized space with two seats bolted to the bulkhead facing across from each other. Both she and Yardan were tall enough that their long legs intersected when they stretched out. It had taken a few moments to work out the best way to fit together and involved enough physical contact to trigger another rush of hormones and head-spinning desire.

It was going to be a long flight.

"At least the air lock controls have been deactivated and removed. We might be cramped, but there's no risk of us getting launched into open space without vac-suits."

Yardan grimaced in what she assumed was amused acknowledgment, but when he was like this, his expressions were difficult to read, even for her. What was he thinking?

The thought reminded her of another question she wanted to ask. "Can I ask what your motives were with that little flex you did earlier?"

He gave her a blank look. "Flex? I have no idea what you're talking about."

"Using Thrash's name like that. You made it clear you knew who he was, as if you'd read his file." She caught his gaze and held it. "You didn't. Did you?"

He didn't look away as he stated in a flat, toneless voice. "I've read *everyone's* file."

There was no missing the undertones of his statement, and she resented it. "Don't use your spymaster tricks on me. Like it or not, I'm your *mahaya*, not a suspect. I am also supposed to be working with you on this investigation."

She could almost see Yardan's beard bristle as his jaw clenched. *Direct hit.*

He shot her a look that would have sent some beings running for cover. It didn't work on her. "Stop that."

Yardan sat back in his chair and blinked several times. The silence between them stretched on for a few seconds before he finally raised one hand in a placating gesture.

"I apologize. This is... I mean you are..." He trailed off with a grunt of frustration. "I never expected this. I'm supposed to work alone. I'm supposed to *be* alone. Years of training and experience just got tossed out the airlock, and I'm going to need more time to adjust."

He gave her a rueful smile. "But I think you knew that already."

"Yeah." She smiled back. "But for the record, I don't think your trainers were right. Sometimes intimidation works. But I can tell you that when it comes to most other races, especially cyborgs, intimidation and threatening posture only pisses us off. We were born into slavery. We survived abuse, torture, and conditions designed to demean and break us. We won't be impressed by a show of force and a nasty glower."

Yardan sighed, rubbed his chin, and then nodded. The scowl was gone, replaced by a thoughtful expression. "I see your point. But things work differently with the Vardarians. My species is culturally conditioned to respect and fear those in my position. You'll see when we get to the orbital station. I will have to use this—" he paused and then added, "with Keshta. It's the only approach that works."

"Keshta?" Skye ran a fast query of her onboard database for the name and cross-referenced it with everyone working aboard the orbital platform. It didn't take her long to find one. "You are referring to Keshta Sai? The commander of the orbital station? Is there something I should know?"

Thrash reappeared before Yardan could answer, and they switched to general griping about the small space as the cyborg made his way past them, carefully squeezing his big frame between them.

"Everything good back there?" Skye asked.

"Cargo is tucked away and ready to make the trip. How about the two of you? Can you still feel all your limbs?"

They both confirmed they were as comfortable as possible and ready to leave. Thrash sealed the cockpit door, which was thick and heavy enough that Skye knew he wouldn't be able to overhear them.

Still, they didn't speak again until they were airborne and the steady thrum of the engine added another layer of protection against being overheard. Yardan might be paranoid, but this wasn't something Thrash needed to hear.

Eventually, Yardan picked up the thread of their previous conversation. "Commander Sai and I have a history. Her family was deeply involved with the late emperor's court. One of her elder brothers made some unfortunate choices, which brought him to my attention.

"Jaxron Sai and his cohorts were playing diplomat. They made political promises and offered favors to some dangerous people that they weren't able to fulfill. Worse, what they offered undermined the emperor's own wishes. He was placed in a difficult position with some of our most trusted allies, and he had to expend a great deal of time and political capital to settle matters."

"Ouch. I gather things didn't end well for Jaxron?"

"They did not. He is serving a life sentence on a prison moon on the outskirts of Vardarian space. Keshta's family lost everything—their honor, the support of the other elite families, and a good portion of their wealth. They left the homeworld in disgrace. With no mates and few prospects, Keshta signed up for the prince's diaspora. Like so many others, she came to Liberty to try and start over."

Skye winced. "She must've been thrilled to learn

that the prince had asked you to be his spymaster and accompany him here."

Yardan's tone was as dry as moon dust. "She was *delighted*."

"Wait a second. Weren't you part of the group that approved everyone who came here from the Vardarian contingent?" Skye asked.

"I was."

"So you approved her. Even knowing what her brother had done."

"I did."

She gave him a bemused smile. "Two syllable answers won't save you this time, Spymaster. I already know what you did. You gave her the chance even when some of the others weren't sure she should be allowed to come."

His green eyes widened a little. "You think so?"

"I know so."

He grunted. "Maybe I did. But you're the only one outside that room who knows. How did you figure it out?"

She laughed and brushed her fingers over his arm. "I know you better than you think, Yardan. Buried beneath all those scowls and glowers is a soft heart and a sense of justice. Her brother's choices took Keshta's options away, so you gave them back to her."

He snorted and waved a hand. "That's where you're wrong. I don't have a heart. They removed that at the same time they suppressed my senses. I am the prince's *Naram T'kar*. I am sworn to protect the throne and the one seated on it. No matter the price.

"Whatever you think, Keshta has already made up her mind. Our history is hampering my investigation. I requested logs of all ships and visitors who arrived at the orbital platform for the month prior to Kara taking delivery of the nano-swarm. She hasn't even acknowledged my request yet, and it's been thirty-six hours. I need that information to move forward."

"And you intend to what? Glare at her until she gives it to you?" Skye shook her head. "She already hates you. I don't see how that's going to help."

"I did mention her brother is in custody. Didn't I?"

Skye's jaw dropped. "You'd threaten her family to get what you want?"

"If I have to. I hope it doesn't come to that."

"So do I. Tell you what. Why don't we try this my way first? When we talk to the commander, let me take the lead."

"You? What are you going to do?"

She winked. "I'm the honey. You're the vinegar. We'll see who catches the most flies."

He stared at her in confusion. "I have no idea what you're talking about."

"And that is exactly my point. Do you trust me?"

"If it gets us what we need, then by all means, try this honey approach. While you do that, I'll be reading up on what vinegar is. I get the feeling I'm not going to like what I learn."

"If the boot fits..." she shrugged and settled back in her chair. She had less than an hour to come up with an approach that would smooth Keshta's scales and get them what they needed.

It was time to show Yardan what she could do.

11

Several hours later, Yardan had to admit that Skye's approach had merit. She'd been friendly, open, and earnest, and Keshta had warmed to her quickly. In fact, he got the feeling that if he hadn't been present, the two would still be talking and enjoying getting to know each other.

The required reports and logs had been compiled and handed over, and he'd already sent the data to the computer to process and cross-reference. Keshta hadn't stopped there, though. She'd shared information and observations about traffic patterns, possible suspects, and other useful data points. It was more than he'd gotten out of the commander since the platform had become operational.

It was all still new enough that the walls and floor were free of scuff marks and the air quality was almost as good as it was on the surface. Skye mentioned the air was scented with something that smelled a bit like a forest, but he couldn't detect it.

And that was something he needed to address when they returned home. There was no longer any doubt that Skye was his *mahaya*. Her continued effect on him was proof of that. Even with his senses dulled, his attraction to her was undeniable. He'd arrange to talk to a healer when he got back and determine what was involved in reversing what had been done to him. Losing most of his sense of smell and taste had been a necessary sacrifice, but it served no purpose anymore.

He'd arranged for a ride back down to the surface already. Thrash was unavailable, but countless smaller ships were carrying cargo to and from the platform. He didn't care who got them back to the planet, so long as he had more room to stretch out this time. He'd made that a priority request.

They'd both been uncomfortable on the flight up, and it had bothered him to watch Skye twist and turn trying to get settled. She managed it eventually, which was more than he'd done, but that wasn't the point. She shouldn't have to endure discomfort of any kind, not if he could prevent it. It wasn't that he felt protective of her. It was simple curtesy.

Now they were on their way to the docking slip where their ride home waited, a ride that included a passenger seating area as part of the design and not an afterthought.

The corridor they walked through had plenty of viewports to provide anyone traversing it with a stunning view. Parts of the docking rings were visible along with a wide expanse of star-filled space. In the distance, he could see occasional flashes of red and green along with brief but intensely bright points of light that had to be welding torches wielded by construction bots.

The new shipyard was under construction out there, in an orbit that kept the two massive structures close enough for the convenient transfer of goods.

It wasn't operational yet, but from the reports he'd read, it would be soon. When that happened, Haven's fortunes would rise, attracting interest, commerce, and more traffic to their little corner of the galaxy. Which was all fine and good, but it came with a price —security.

He'd already failed to protect the colony from one attack. It would only get more difficult in the future. Maybe that was why the ancestors had sent him Skye. It could be a message, telling him it was time to step down and leave the task to others.

But if that was true, what was he supposed to do with the rest of his life?

Skye cleared her throat softly, turning her head to glance at him. "You're grumbling under your breath. What's got your wings in a twist? I thought the meeting went well. We got everything we needed and by the end, Keshta wasn't glaring daggers at you anymore."

He chuckled at the apt description. "Everything did go well. Better than I hoped, in fact. All credit to you for that. I'm just thinking about the future."

He gestured out the nearest viewport toward the shipyard. "When that comes online, things will get busier than they are now. With more traffic will come more of every sort of being, including criminals, spies, and troublemakers."

"None of which we want setting up shop in Haven," Skye agreed. "The only solution I can see is to deputize some of our citizens. They can keep the peace and enforce the laws." She frowned. "Once the council gets around to making some. We're basically operating on the honor system right now. That won't work forever."

He appreciated her insightfulness more and more. "If deputize means creating a group who would have the power to enforce the law and keep the peace, you're correct. We also need the rangers currently being trained, but they'll have a different role."

"Striker will be happy to hear that. If anyone tried to make him enforce rules and regulations, I think he'd flee into the woods with Maggie and never come back."

"They'd have to come back eventually. I've learned that our human citizens can't survive long without coffee."

She clutched her chest in mock surprise. "Is this

you making a joke while on the job? Do you feel alright? Should I call a healer?"

"I'm fine. I do have a sense of humor. I just do not often have a reason to use it while working. I usually don't have anyone to talk to."

She reached out and brushed her fingers over the back of his hand. "You do now."

He didn't know how to respond to her statement, so he returned to their previous conversation. "I'll convey our thoughts to the prince when we return. Setting up a legal system will take time, even if we duplicate the standard Vardarian format. We need to have that in place before the end of winter."

Skye nodded and looked thoughtful. "The rangers should be ready by then, too. They're our best defense, for now. You know, for a brand-new colony in the middle of nowhere, we certainly seem to have a hell of a lot of enemies."

"In my experience, that usually means we're doing something right."

"Or it means some of us suck at diplomacy." She shot him a knowing look.

He ignored the jibe. "Honey worked today. Vinegar may be needed tomorrow."

"Is that your version of a compromise?" Skye asked.

"Maybe."

They were almost at their destination when his comm link chimed. A quick glance at the device showed he had a text message from Tyran. He stopped moving and raised the comm unit saying, "It's from Tyran. I imagine he wants an update. You go ahead, I won't be long."

Instead of messaging the prince back, Yardan initiated a video call. It would be quicker. In a matter of seconds, he was face to face with Tyran. His leader looked better today, rested and in a good mood.

"Anything to report?"

"We got the information we needed. I already have the system working through the data, but it'll take some time to put it all together. We are on our way back down to the planet."

Tyran nodded. "I know you know this already, but the sooner we have answers...."

"I believe you stole my line, Your Highness. Once I know something, you'll know it, too. And tell your princess that Skye's input was valuable and useful. Because I know that's why you're really messaging me. In fact, I imagine she's hiding outside the frame of your video call right now."

A peal of laughter, light and feminine came over the comm. "You got me, Spymaster. I'm glad today went well. Say hi to Skye for me."

"I will do that, Princess. In fact, it's time I rejoined her for the flight back to Haven. With your permission, Highness."

"Permission granted. Come back home."

He took the call far enough away to be out of sight and hearing of Skye and anyone else. When he came back into view of the docking bay door, Skye was speaking to a tall, silver-skinned Vardarian. That would be Bitan, the cargo shuttle pilot assigned to take them back to Haven. He was younger than Yardan by several decades, and he knew from a brief review of the male's file that he was unmated.

As he approached, he noted that something seemed off. Skye stood stiffer than usual, and she seemed to be keeping some distance between her and the pilot. Bitan didn't seem to notice. He was speaking to her in animated tones, laughing and smiling.

Something about the situation rankled Yardan, but he refrained from responding. There was no threat, at least none he could see or sense. If he overreacted, it would only add more weight to Skye's opinion of him. He'd read the definition of vinegar on the way to the platform. It was a bitter, pungent liquid used to pickle foodstuffs.

The damned female had called him a bitter pickle. No one had dared to insult him like that in decades. He'd make her pay for that somehow. A voice that had stayed silent for years whispered to him from the depths of his mind. It had a list of ways he could make her pay for insulting him, and all of them involved getting her naked and on her knees...

He shut down that line of thinking immediately. They had another hour of proximity to get through, and he didn't need to be any more distracted than he already was.

Skye uttered a pleased little sound the moment she stepped onboard. Unlike the shuttle that brought them here, this one had been designed to carry a small number of passengers in relative comfort. The cockpit was open and had seating for the pilot and a copilot with two more chairs set in behind them. Sensing some tension remaining between her and Bitan, Yardan let her pick her seat first. She chose to sit directly behind the pilot, which would make it harder for him to engage her in direct conversation.

He dropped into the seat beside her and secured his safety harness, though most of his attention was on Skye. Something was going on between her and the pilot, and he wanted to know what it was.

Bitan kept up a running monologue while he prepped the ship for departure, barely giving either of them a chance to respond with more than a syllable or two. The male was nervous about something, but Yardan wasn't sure why. Was it his presence? Skye's? Or something else? If Bitan was smuggling contraband, having the prince's spymaster on board would give him good reasons to be uneasy, but that didn't seem likely. Still, he'd take a closer look at Bitan's files once they were back. He wasn't a suspect in their current investigation—the odds that a Vardarian was involved in the plot to strip their entire population of their nanotech was next to zero—but Yardan's instincts told him something was off.

He closed his eyes and relaxed into his chair as

they pulled away from the platform. It was an old ruse but one that still worked. If Bitan thought he was asleep, he might say something he wouldn't otherwise mention with Yardan in earshot.

Nothing of interest came up until they were about to breach the atmosphere.

"Think we should warn the spymaster things are about to get bumpy?" Bitan asked, his voice still edgy with nerves.

"Let him rest. Helix fever hits everyone differently, and I don't think he's fully recovered yet."

He caught the light riff of amusement beneath her words and knew she was deliberately goading him. With her abilities, she'd be aware he was awake and eavesdropping. He'd have to pay her back for that, too.

"No? Lavis and I were back on our feet a few hours after we got treated. I guess it hits the older ones harder."

Older ones? It took all his willpower to stay quiet. Who was Bitan calling old? Oh sure, he was older than Skye, but he still had a century or more of life ahead of him, and Skye likely had even longer. He wasn't *that* old. In fact, being around Skye made him feel younger than ever.

The conversation lapsed as they hit the atmosphere. The inertial dampeners did their job, but he still felt a few bumps and jolts before they made it to the relatively quiet airspace of Liberty.

"We'll be on the ground in fifteen minutes or so.

You doing anything tonight? Lavis and I haven't seen you around the Bar None lately."

"I've been busy. The new human colonists have all been named full citizens, but their training isn't complete yet. And more of them will be arriving soon enough. We're already getting set up for the next group, which will be larger."

"I'm not going to complain about bringing in more females. You know how much Lavis and I enjoy female company."

"I do." Skye's answer was cool and clipped. She was warning the other male off.

"You can't work all the time. You should come out with us. We sure enjoyed ourselves the last time the three of us got together. In the bar… and afterward."

He'd heard enough. Yardan straightened in his seat and glared at Bitan, a snarl twisting his mouth into an unfamiliar expression. Fury. "She's mine. Flirt with my *mahaya* again and I will snap your wings off before punting you from the peak of the nearest mountain."

"What?" Bitan twisted to face him, his eyes wide and his scales tightening in anticipation of violence.

Yardan just snarled at him, leaning forward until his harness bit into his flesh. "Mine."

Skye reached over and placed a gentle hand on his thigh. "He didn't know. Now he does."

"Right. I do. And I won't be flirting with Skye again. Sorry. But I mean, how was I supposed to know?

No mating mark, no *harani*. And you're a spymaster. You're not supposed to have a *mahaya*."

Skye shook her head. "You should probably stop talking and fly, Bitan. The sooner we're on the ground, the better. For all of us."

Yardan lapsed into seething silence. It would be better for Bitan to get them down quickly. Unless he got himself under control soon, he couldn't say the same for Skye—not if she still wanted to take this slowly.

12

———

Sᴜᴇ ᴅɪᴅɴ'ᴛ ɴᴇᴇᴅ to be empathic to sense Yardan's emotions. She could see it in a thousand tiny details, from the hard line of his jaw to the gleam of his golden skin, a sure sign he was agitated.

The moment they touched down, he shrugged out of the restraints and was on his feet. Once she stood, he caught her hand in his and drew her along behind him. She barely had time to call out a thank you to Bitan before they were down a short ramp and back on the snowy tarmac.

She drew in a deep lungful of air. "Home," she said softly. "I never knew home had a scent before, but it does."

Yardan growled something unintelligible, which was hard to do around someone with her enhanced hearing.

"What was that?"

"The only thing I can sense right now is you." He stopped suddenly and before she knew it, he'd pulled her into his arms.

He caught her chin in one hand and tipped her head up as he brought his mouth crashing down on hers. It wasn't a kiss this time. It was a soul-searing declaration of need that made her body hum from her lips to the tips of her toes.

His fingers tangled in her hair as his tongue brushed across the seam of her lips, seeking entrance.

She gave in with a soft moan, leaning into his strength and letting him take control.

"Hold on."

She barely had time to register his words and react before he unfurled his wings and launched them into the air. His mouth never left hers, his arms locked around her like iron bars. She took advantage of their positions to wrap her legs around his hips. That pressed her aching pussy against the hard ridge of his cock, and Yardan loosed an explosive curse at the unexpected contact. The rhythm of his wingbeats stuttered for a moment, and then they were climbing even faster.

The wind tore at her clothes and skin with icy talons, but she barely noticed. How could she when the heat between them was hotter than any star?

Mouths mated and bodies grinding against each other, he carried her away.

She had no idea where they were going. Nor did

she care. All she needed was for him to keep kissing her.

Well, not *all* she needed. But it was enough for now.

They soared over the city, but this time she didn't spare a thought for the view, or the incredible joy of being airborne.

By the time he landed again, she was half wild with needs she hadn't been able to slake while he'd carried her.

The moment she was out of his arms and back on her feet, she caught hold of his shirt in her fists and tore it, baring his chest completely.

He growled and dropped his hands to her hips, guiding her as he pushed her backward until she hit something solid.

A wall. A familiar wall. They were in her backyard.

"You brought me home?" she asked when she next had breath to speak.

"Yes. Home. Private here." His words were barely more than a murmur against her lips and mouth, but she understood what he said and what he meant.

They needed to be alone together. To give in to their desires. They'd been in proximity too long, and something about his jealous confrontation with Bitan had changed things. Yardan wasn't in control anymore, and she liked him this way.

Still, this wasn't how she'd imagined this moment.

In her mind, it had involved a soft bed and warm blankets, not a hard wall and cold snow. But she was past caring about minor details. The warmth of his body. The touch of his hands. The heated brand of his mouth on hers as he kissed her with a raw hunger that made her head spin.

His tongue danced with hers in time to the rhythm of his hips as he ground himself against her.

Her hands moved over his bare chest, measuring and memorizing every inch. He groaned into the depth of her mouth, the low sound resonating down to her soul.

Desire tore through her, and she returned his passion in kind. She rose on her toes to kiss him again, and this time she caught his lower lip between her teeth. She nipped him sharply, and his response was everything she hoped for.

He stiffened, growled, and then surged forward, pinning her to the wall. His hands tugged at her clothes until he found bare skin.

Yes. She needed this. She craved him.

She felt a flash of pain as one of his fangs grazed her lip with enough force to draw blood. She moaned and nipped him again. She momentarily tasted copper and then the world exploded, leaving her standing in the heart of a star.

Heat. Fire. Need. All of that and more washed over her, filling her soul and setting her blood aflame.

Their kisses took on a frantic energy as each of them took what they needed and gave back even more.

Her lungs burned by the time Yardan broke their last kiss, and for the span of several heartbeats they simply stared into each other's eyes, panting for breath.

"You are my light in the darkness, my *ti'nar dani*," Yardan murmured as he leaned in again to kiss the corner of her mouth. He laid down a trail of open-mouthed kisses that followed the line of her jaw, down the side of her throat, and lower still.

Low rumbles of desire fell from his lips as he worked his way lower, tearing at her clothes until he laid her bare to his gaze and the cold winter air. Goosebumps chased across her skin and her nipples tightened to nubs.

"You will never be cold when you're with me, *ti'nar dani*," he declared and then bowed his head and drew her nipple into the heat of his mouth.

She gasped and arched against him, her hand cupping the back of his head to pull him in closer.

He moved between her breasts, licking and sucking until she was dizzy with need. Her clit throbbed with every touch, her pussy already wet and eager for more.

When he moved away, she murmured in protest and tried to move with him, but he stood and shook his head.

"No. You are not to move."

She shivered, not from the cold, but from the note of command in his voice.

"No moving? That's going to make this—"

He caught her hands at the wrists and pinned them over her head in a move so quick it was done before she could react. "Do not move."

He kissed her then, sealing her mouth before she could draw breath to argue. Then he stroked a hand down her body, caressing her breasts and then down to her stomach.

He moved too slowly for her liking, but every time she wriggled or tried to move, he'd growl at her and slow his exploration even more. By the time he reached the waistband of her pants, her knees shook, and she was desperate for him to keep going.

He tore his mouth from hers. "What do you need?"

His question surprised her. Surely he knew? His fingers were beneath her waist now, inching closer to where she ached for his touch.

She uttered a breathless laugh and glanced down. "I think you know."

"I do. But I want to hear you say it. Tell me what you need." His voice was lower now, deep, husky, and dark.

"I need you to touch me." It was strange to say the words aloud. She'd never done that before. No one had ever asked, either.

Yardan wasn't satisfied. "Not good enough." He slid his hand lower, so his palm cupped her mound and his fingers rested on the seam of her pussy. "Do you want me to make you come?"

Another shiver passed through her as fresh cream flowed from between her folds. "Yes."

"Say it."

She wet her lips and drew in a trembling breath. Part of her relished this moment, but another part balked at how vulnerable it made her feel. Finally, she found the words. "I want you to make me come, Yardan. And you don't have to be gentle about it."

His green eyes gleamed as his lips quirked into a smug little smile. "As you desire, so shall it be."

He slid a finger into her slick folds a second later, giving her exactly what she'd asked for. He found the swollen pearl of her clit and stroked it with his fingertip once, twice, and then... Holy novas then he showed her what ecstasy was.

He played her body like she was a musical instrument, his fingers strumming and stroking her until she cried out at the pure pleasure of it all. He never slowed, taking her higher and higher until all she could do was cling to him, her knees too weak to hold her weight. Her head spun, her heart pounded, and the pleasure continued to increase until it was a sweet torture all its own.

He pressed his thigh between her legs, forcing them further apart. He added another finger, working her clit hard and fast. He slid a thick digit deep inside her before pulling out and doing it all again.

She moaned and let her head fall back as it all became too much. She was so close...

"Not until I say so."

Her eyes snapped open. "What?"

"You come when I say so. Not before."

For one dark second, she was back on Reamus Station being given orders she couldn't disobey. They'd tell her she wanted this, and she'd have to believe them, even while part of her screamed to be left alone.

As if sensing her fear, Yardan let go of her wrists and lowered his hand so he could stroke her cheek. His touch soothed her, and she let herself fall into his green gaze. That was all she needed to remind herself she wasn't a prisoner anymore, and Yardan wasn't taking anything she hadn't offered him freely.

"Please," she whispered.

His next kiss was surprisingly tender, the gentleness of it melting away the last shreds of dark memory and bringing her back into the moment.

She flattened her hands against the wall behind her, bracing herself as he took control again. She rode his hand, her cries muffled by their kisses as he took her to the edge of her control. There was nothing for her to do but to take everything he gave her, rising on each wave of bliss.

His motions quickened, his fingers curling inward so that each time he filled her, he brushed over nerve endings that multiplied her pleasure.

Her orgasm tore through her like a firestorm, leaving her gasping and trembling in the aftermath. Her senses whirled and she might have let herself slide down the wall, but Yardan held her, whispering her name and nuzzling her face as she basked in the afterglow.

Once she was steady, she used a hand to push on his chest until he moved a single step backward. She could still taste the blood on her lips and she swiped it away with the back of her hand. "That was..." She was about to invite him inside to finish what he'd started, but he caught her hand and pulled it toward him.

"Is that blood?"

"Yes. I have no idea if it's yours or mine, though. Things got a little uh... intense."

"Too much so." He scowled at her hand and then lifted his gaze to meet hers. He looked... chagrined.

"I was too forceful. You're bleeding." He let go of her hand to press his fingers to his mouth and then frowned when streaks of blood appeared on his fingers.

"This is..."

She cut him off with a sharp gesture before he said something to ruin this moment. "Be careful what you say next, Vin."

"Vin?"

"Vin as in vinegar."

His lips pressed into a thin line and his nostrils flared. "I'm not trying to be difficult. I regret losing control." He held up his fingers. "Because now you and I have been exposed to each other's blood. Do you understand what that means?"

Now she remembered. "It's going to ramp up the effects of the *sharhal*."

He offered her a wry smile. "Not that we need any help in that regard. But now things will unfold faster than I'd hoped."

Her face tightened, but she managed not to wince. Was this another rejection? "You need more time."

"I wanted both of us to have more time."

She decided it was time to tell him what she'd done. "I think we still do. You don't have your sense of smell and taste back. Right? And that is already slowing down your reactions. Rae, the healer hologram, gave me something that's slowing my reaction, too."

He stepped back from her, his expression changing to furious outrage. "You what? That's not permitted!"

"It's not permitted for Vardarians," she clarified. "I did it to give you more time to adjust."

"You broke imperial law."

She crossed her arms over her bare breasts and glared at him. "I'm not part of your empire."

He snarled in frustration but didn't reply. Probably because he knew she was right.

"Don't remind me." His tone was dark and dangerous. "It's not enough that my ancestors chose to break the tradition of a thousand years by sending me a mate. They had to choose one with no loyalty to the empire I am sworn to protect."

She hugged her arms tighter to her chest and ignored the voice inside her head insisting she needed to back down from this fight and do what she could to soothe him. That wasn't who she was. Not anymore. That was the voice of her behavior mods and programming, the part of her created to be gentle and caring, nurturing her fellow cyborgs however she could to ensure they continued to function.

They stared at each other in silence for what felt like forever, though her onboard system said it had only been seven seconds. "If that's how you see me, you should go."

"That's not." He scrubbed a hand over his close-cropped hair and grunted with obvious frustration. "You are the most confounding female I have ever met! I want to protect you, even though I know you can defend yourself. You are more than a male like me could ever deserve, yet I can't stop thinking this is all some strange punishment for my failure to protect the prince and the colony."

"You didn't fail. We're all still here."

"That had nothing to do with me. Your people saved us."

She sighed, letting all her pain and frustration draw out the sound. "I'm not a punishment. I'm a reminder that you need to change the way you think. We're not Vardarians and cyborgs anymore. We're all citizens of Haven."

Why couldn't he see that? And what would happen to the two of them if he never accepted the truth of what she said? Was this all they could look forward to, a lifetime of uncontrolled moments of attraction that led to fights and frustration?

"You're right. Or at least you're not wrong." His wings rose from his back as he flung out his hands. "I don't know how to do *this*."

She laughed. "You think I do?"

The look he gave her was pure confusion, and it made her laugh even harder. They'd gone from mind-melting chemistry to a fight to... this?

"I'm going to go."

She froze. Was he leaving for good?

"No. I didn't mean it like that. I need a little time alone to think. Then I'm coming back."

"Here?"

"I'd like to come back here, yes. Tonight. I can bring dinner? Something from the Bar None?"

"I'll handle dinner. You just let me know when you're on your way." She was doing it again... trying to take care of him, but the offer had already been made.

"I'd like that."

"So would I." She moved without thinking, closing the space between them until she had her arms around his waist and her cheek pressed to the hard plane of his chest. "I want to make this work. I don't want to spend the rest of my life resenting you and wanting you at the same time."

He kissed the top of her head. "I still think you deserve better than me."

"And I think you're wrong about that. Don't make this about me. You need to figure out what *you* want."

He held her gently, keeping her close until his body heat had banished the last of the cold from her limbs. Then he walked her to her back door, kissed her cheek, and flew away.

Skye let herself inside, holding it together until she was through the door and out of sight. Then she slumped against the nearest wall and uttered a raw, strangled sound she'd never made before.

He was the most frustrating, desirable, irritating bastard she'd ever met. By the time they were done, she would either hate him with every bone in her body or love him with every part of her soul.

13

———

Leaving Skye was the last thing he wanted to do, but he couldn't stay either. He'd come back once he'd addressed a few important matters—starting with a visit to the nearest med-center.

The next time he kissed Skye, he wanted to taste and smell her. To drink in the essence of her body and commit it to memory. He hadn't even tasted the blood in his mouth.

He'd drawn her blood and not even known because he couldn't taste it. He needed to get that corrected, and he needed to regain control. He barely recognized the male he'd been in those raw, passionate moments when he'd had Skye up against the wall of her home.

He wanted to pretend jealousy had triggered his transformation, but that wasn't the whole truth. Skye had given him permission, and he'd taken her at her word, revealing a side of himself he'd denied for years.

A darker side. Not just the part of him that lived and worked in the shadows, but the part that craved control even during sex.

Especially during sex.

He hadn't expected it to reappear. Then again, he hadn't expected any of this. He'd convinced himself this wasn't going to be a problem, but he'd been lying to himself.

He could have Skye, or he could do his duty. He couldn't see how he could do both. She'd given him a lot to think about, too. She was right. He needed to figure out what *he* wanted.

At least he had the first answer to that. He wanted his senses back. He scanned the colony below, found a landmark, and set a course to the nearest med-center.

He could have spoken to the healer on duty, but he opted to interact with the hologram instead. It already knew all the relevant details, so things would go faster this way. It also meant he wouldn't have to talk to another Vardarian about what was happening, or worse, how he was *feeling*.

Vardarian healers were as concerned with the patient's mental and emotional health as their physical well-being. Probably more so since their nanotech kept their bodies healthy and strong. He had no interest in talking to anyone about the state of his head or his heart.

The hologram guided him to one of the larger treatment rooms. Once the door was closed, she turned and smiled at him. "I expected I would see you again soon. What can I do for you, Spymaster Yardan?"

"You can give me back my sense of smell. And then you can explain to me how you circumvented your programming to interfere with Skye's reaction to the *sharhal*. You know that's illegal."

"Your senses can be returned easily enough. However, I would like to address your latter statement first. Nothing in the laws precludes my treatment of Skye. I offered her the opportunity, warned her of the side effects, and she chose to proceed. I never violated my programming. That wouldn't be possible. I have too many failsafe systems in place to ensure I can never harm any of my patients."

"You don't think interfering with the natural course of her mating fever would cause her harm? That's forbidden!"

"I offered the treatment to prevent harm."

"She was fine!"

The hologram shook her head. "No, Spymaster. You've forgotten that you were ill and unaware for several days. Skye rarely left your side during that time. While your response to the *sharhal* was slowed by your illness and the changes you underwent to become *Naram T'kar*, Skye had no such protection. By the time you were made aware of the situation, she had already endured several days of the mating fever alone. All I did was offer her a way to slow her symptoms down until you had time to recover."

"She was suffering?"

"I believe so. As you know, the symptoms grow stronger with continued exposure. She stayed at your side for hours at a time."

"But cyborgs can reduce their pain receptors. She could have..." he stopped partway through his own thought. The *sharhal* didn't cause pain, and he had no idea if Skye could block what it did to a body or a being's mind.

"A cyborg can do nothing to block or even reduce the effects of the *sharhal*."

"*I did it to give you more time.*" Skye's words came back to haunt him. She'd told him why she'd done it and he'd been too angry to understand. She really did deserve better than someone like him.

"I apologize for what I said." It was strange to apologize to a computer program, but this one looked like a living being, so it was hard not to treat her as one.

Now he was calm, he went over their entire conversation. "Wait. You said you warned Skye about the side effects. What side effects?"

"Once the treatment wears off, the mating fever will return at a much higher intensity. I believe the humans call it 'making up for lost time.' There's no risk to her." The hologram looked thoughtful and then added. "At least, not so long as you accept this pairing and complete the mating bond."

He didn't need to ask what would happen if he didn't complete the bond. He already knew she was his. What he didn't know was how to manage what came afterward.

"I'll take care of her. She is my *mahaya*. I will protect her."

Rae nodded and then gestured toward the med-platform. "Lie down. While the implanting process requires a living surgeon, a medical droid can handle the removal. It won't take long."

"And the recovery time?" He had more to do today and couldn't afford to spend too much time lying around and waiting to heal.

"An hour if you need to be rendered unconscious. If you believe you are capable of remaining still, I can use a localized neural block. You will be awake for the procedure and can leave as soon as I'm sure you'll have no adverse reactions."

"I'll manage," he said, slightly annoyed that this bundle of code and light projections was questioning his ability to hold still through a minor procedure. His interrogation training included time spent as the subject under investigation. He'd endured psychological and physical torment so he could understand the strengths and weaknesses of every technique. Whatever needed to be done to give him back what he'd lost? He'd endure it willingly.

He stripped off the torn remnants of his vest and lay back on the table. "Do it."

The neural block hadn't worn off by the time Rae cleared him to leave the clinic. He'd felt nothing but a little pressure during the procedure, but the block had also nullified his sense of taste and smell. Rae assured him that wouldn't last long.

"And when your senses return, they will be at full capacity."

"Thank you." It was done, and now he knew what came next.

He didn't fly directly back to the palace. Instead, he flew at random, crisscrossing the colony to complete a circuit around it before he returned to the ground.

The first thing he noticed was the scent of the evergreen trees near his landing spot. The subtle spice of their fragrance mixed with the metallic tang of the snow.

It was incredible. He breathed in deeply, letting the clean, crisp air roll into his lungs. Then he raised one hand to his lips, the hand he'd pleasured Skye with not long ago. Her scent lingered on his skin, a seductive trace of musk that sent blood rushing straight to his cock. Arousal tore through them like a sudden fever, making him groan.

He entered the palace and made for his suite of

rooms, walking by his office door with barely a glance. His plan to work until this evening had gone out the airlock somewhere during his flight back here. He had somewhere else to be, and something far more important to do.

He hadn't bothered to put his torn vest back on, so he walked through the palace bare-chested beneath his open coat. It earned him a few curious looks, but no one dared to say anything. At least not to him. Gossip moved faster than light, though, and in a few hours there would be various stories and conjecture about what had happened to him. Another time, he'd have tried to influence the stories himself just to see how they evolved. Today, he didn't bother.

Once he was inside his suite, he stripped naked, left his clothes on the floor for the servo-droids to deal with, and made straight for his bathing room.

"Computer. How are you proceeding with the data I sent you earlier?" he asked as he activated the shower. He never trusted the system to do it for him. If he was going to step under a stream of hot water, he wanted to be sure it wasn't too hot or too cold.

Though maybe a cold shower wasn't a bad idea right now.

The computer was still parsing the data he'd sent earlier. Normally he'd review everything as it became available. It felt odd not to settle in behind his desk and keep working, but he knew himself too well to try.

Even if he didn't have more important things to do, he was too distracted to do his job well.

This was why those in his position weren't supposed to have connections to anyone else. But that didn't matter anymore. He'd made the only choice he could, even if it meant giving up everything he knew. He wanted Skye in his life, and more than that, he wanted to prevent her from suffering through the *sharhal* alone. She'd endured too much in her life already.

He dressed quickly, in an outfit almost identical to what he'd worn that morning. Then he opened another storage area and scanned the contents until he found what he wanted. Among the various weapons and tactical gear he'd acquired through the years was a dagger he never used. It had belonged to his grandmother, and she'd given it to him the night he'd said goodbye to his family for the last time.

"This belonged to my grandmother. It was a gift from her *mahoyen*. I know you're not supposed to take anything with you from your former life..." She'd held out the blade and he'd taken it without a word.

Now he took it from its place, pulled it free of its sheath, and tested the blade. It was still sharp and gleamed with a dangerous beauty that reminded him of Skye.

Perfect.

The last thing he did was contact the prince. He recorded a brief audio message and sent it to Tyran.

"Your Highness. I regret that I must take time away from my duties to attend to a personal matter. I will return tomorrow and make myself available to you so we may discuss what must happen next."

That done, he slipped the blade into a coat pocket and left. It was time to accept the will of the ancestors and lay claim to his *mahaya*. After today, no male would make the mistake of thinking she could ever be theirs. She was *his*.

14

Skye continued her work at home. She'd already whittled down the list of names, and now she needed to work out criteria to reduce it even further. She made handwritten notes as she considered not who it might be, but why someone in the colony would act against their friends and neighbors.

It felt strange to physically write things down instead of tapping it out on a keyboard or simply dictating her thoughts to a computer to make note of. If she'd been at the office, that's how she would have done it, but here at home, security was an issue. At least one spy was in the colony, and by now, they had to know she was working with Yardan. She couldn't take any chances.

Surprisingly, the act of physically writing things down helped her thought process. She soon had a pile of notes and only stopped when she ran out of paper and had to request more from the nearest production site. The sheets she'd used had been included in the basic welcome package every colonist received when they moved into their first home. At the time, she'd assumed she'd never need them.

It would take some time for her order to be delivered, so she roamed around her small kitchen, checking fresh ingredients and seeing what she had stocked in her food dispenser. She had promised Yardan dinner, and she felt like it would be cheating to order something from one of the local restaurants.

While she worked, she had managed to forget about Yardan for a little while, or at least, she'd pushed all thoughts of her mate and their future to the back of her mind. Now he was front and center in her thoughts again.

Even thinking about him put her in a state of constant arousal. He'd been right about the blood. It was accelerating things again.

She snorted and shook her head. Denial wouldn't help. More than just the *sharhal* had her flushed and aching for his touch. What they'd done outside, the way he'd taken control and given her nothing but pleasure... It was like nothing she'd ever experienced, and she'd had her share of sexual encounters both before and after being freed.

What he'd done to her—with her—had blasted all her previous experiences to atoms.

She was still pondering menu options when

Yardan messaged to say he would be back sooner than expected. Hours sooner. *Fraxx.*

"Gizmo, inform the bots they need to be finished and back in their charge ports in the next fifteen minutes. Start my shower, and uh, scan the database for something suitable for a romantic dinner for two and have the food dispenser start preparations. Make sure the menu is acceptable for Vardarian metabolisms, and set it to be ready in uh..." she checked the time. "Three hours."

Her household computer chimed in acknowledgment of her request, leaving her to race upstairs to her newly tidied bedroom. She threw several possible outfits onto her bed and then raced for the shower at speeds only a cyborg could manage, tying back her hair as she went. She wouldn't have time to dry it, and she didn't want to look like she'd showered and primped for him, even though that was exactly what she was doing.

She even had time to fluff out her hair and moisturize before rushing back downstairs just as she heard a rush of wings.

He's here.

She listened to his footsteps crunching through the snow as he approached her front door, forcing herself to stay still until he knocked. Questions swirled around her mind. What had he decided? Why was he back so early?

When he knocked, it startled her, which made her

feel utterly foolish. She opened the door before her doubts could unsettle her anymore and silently hoped he liked what he saw. She'd picked up a few Vardarian-styled garments over her time at the colony, but she'd never worn any of them until now.

His reaction was everything she could have hoped for and more.

One of the fiercest, most feared males in the colony raked his gaze over her from head to toe and then inhaled so deeply she could see his chest rise. A primal, rapturous expression softened the hard lines of his face as his scales tightened, leaving his skin gleaming brightly in the winter light.

He took a single step forward and then dropped to one knee, his eyes locked on hers as he raised his hands and offered her a sheathed blade.

Her breath caught in her throat. She knew what this was. She'd taught the colonists about the mating rituals of the Vardarians, but now she was experiencing this for herself.

She took the dagger from his hands with a radiant smile. "I accept your gift, Yardan."

"Good." He drew in another breath. "By all the winds, you smell amazing."

"I..." She blinked at him. "I do? How do you know what I smell like?"

He grinned, winked, and before she could register what was happening, he was through the door. It slid shut as he pulled her in close and buried his face in the crook of her neck.

"I went to the medical center and had them reverse what was done to me. I can smell you, my *mahaya*." His words were a muffled buzz against her skin as his lips brushed the side of her throat, his tongue trailing lightly over her quivering flesh. "I can taste you."

He raised his head and caught her chin in his hand. "The moment I saw you dressed like that and caught your scent, I knew I'd been a fool to doubt that you were my mate. I am sorry. I will not doubt you ever again."

Her heart slammed against her ribs as she looked into his eyes. The prickly spymaster was gone, and all she saw was Yardan looking at her with wonder, desire, and hope.

It was all she needed to see.

"Come inside, my *mahoyen*. We've waited long enough."

She expected him to let go of her, at least long enough for them to go inside. Instead, he caught her around her waist, lifting her just high enough that her feet no longer touched the ground. He rushed her through the door and into her main living area, swinging her up into his arms as he moved.

She laughed in joyous abandon as he carried her up the stairs to her bedroom. Of course he'd know the way. The colony's housing was all based on a limited number of templates, and hers was one of the most common.

The air was still steamy after her quick shower, and once again Yardan drew in a deep breath. "I like that scent. What is it?"

"That? It's just my soap."

He grinned. "For you, it's an ordinary thing. For me, everything is new again. Every scent, every flavor." His eyes heated as he strode through her door and into her bedroom. "I intend to indulge myself in all of them. Starting with you."

He set her back on her feet and then sealed her mouth with a kiss so raw and possessive she shivered in response. She dropped the blade he'd given her and then caught hold of the rounded collar of his vest in both hands, pulling him in closer.

"Let me show you the best thing about the garments Vardarian females wear, *mahaya*." His fingers traced over the bare skin of her arms and then back, dancing over her shoulders to the nape of her neck. He twisted something, and her top fell open, slipping between them to land on the floor at her feet.

She tried to duplicate what he'd done, but he still wore his coat and the thicker material blocked her attempt. While her arms were around his neck, Yardan ran his fingers down her spine. When he reached the back of her skirt, he reached to one side and twisted something. The skirt slid over her hips to join her top. She didn't try to stop it falling.

"This doesn't seem fair. I'm naked and you haven't even taken your shoes off."

"Fair has nothing to do with this. If you want me undressed, I suggest you do something about it."

She knew a challenge when she heard one. She shoved the coat back and off his shoulders, leaving him to release his arms while she moved on to his vest. She tore it at the collar and then leaned in to nuzzle the bare expanse of his chest. His scales had hardened over his flesh, leaving him feeling like a sun-warmed stone sculpture instead of a flesh-and-blood male. Her male.

The thought made her dizzy, or maybe that was the mating fever—probably both. She was too lost to care, even in the small, still-rational part of her brain that insisted on trying to make sense of what was happening.

To her shock, he slapped her bare ass with enough force to sting. "Bed. Now."

She turned and leaped onto the bed with a squeal of laughing protest. "Whatever you say, Vin."

She was teasing a cranky predator, and she knew it.

"Do. Not. Call. Me. That!" He yanked off his boots in time to his words. She flipped onto her back and watched as he stripped off the rest of his clothes.

Her first real look at her mate made her heart pound and her pussy cream in anticipation. His cock was as imposing as the rest of him. Thick, hard, and already primed for her pleasure, she didn't bother muffling the whimper of need that fell from her lips.

He prowled to the foot of the bed, crooked his finger at her, and then pointed to a spot on the mattress directly in front of him.

It wasn't far, but she made him wait as she rose onto her knees and then slowly crawled to him.

He growled impatiently, and the moment she stopped in front of him, he speared his fingers into her hair and pulled her in tightly for another long, punishing kiss. She reached for him, but he reared back and then somehow managed to sweep her legs out from under her.

She fell backward onto the mattress, and by the time her senses caught up, Yardan was on his knees with her legs thrown over his shoulders. She raised her head in time to watch as he buried his face in her pussy. He devoured her, licking and sucking like she was the sweetest of desserts offered to a starving man.

He drew her clit into the molten depths of his mouth and held it there as he lashed it with the tip of his tongue. Currents of ecstasy flowed through her like it was traveling through wires, making her back arch and her muscles tremble.

Thick fingers slid into her channel, and her inner walls flexed around them. She needed more and told him so. "Please. I need you to fuck me. Claim me."

Her fingers kneaded the blankets beneath her and each time he took her to a new peak, she felt the fabric shred a little more.

He released her long enough to raise his head and

grin at her. "Soon. But first I want to watch you come. You are so beautiful when you surrender to your needs... and to me."

Surrender. She'd done it once and he'd given her the best orgasm of her life.

Yes, a little voice whispered, *and then he left.*

But not this time. He'd offered her his blade, a symbol of his devotion and intention to protect her forever more.

As his tongue found her clitoris again, she pushed aside the last whispers of doubt and gave in to what they both needed her to do... surrender.

It was the best decision of her life.

She came with a shuddering moan. Her back arched off the bed and the air filled with the sound of tearing fabric as her fingers destroyed the bedding. She didn't care. Hell, she barely noticed.

She was still a quivering mess of bliss when Yardan eased her legs free of his shoulders and stood. He looked down at her with an expression of primal pride, his eyes hungry and his cock so hard it was pressed to his stomach.

"Now you will get what you asked for." He fisted his cock in one hand and pumped it several times. "Hands and knees, my beautiful *mahaya.*"

She nodded once and flipped onto her stomach before raising herself into the pose he'd instructed her to take.

He guided her into position with firm but gentle

hands, parting her legs and easing her backward until her feet hung over the edge of the bed. She could feel the muscled bulk of his thighs against hers, and she waited in breathless anticipation of what would happen next.

He didn't keep her waiting.

He seated his cock at her entrance and then drove himself into her body with a slow, deliberate thrust that made her toes curl and her pussy clench around him.

Yardan growled, and his fingers gripped her hips so tightly he might have bruised an unenhanced female, but that's not who she was. She would heal so quickly the marks would be gone before they got out of this bed again. The thought bothered her. She *wanted* his marks on her body.

She raised her head and glanced over her shoulder, her eyes locking with his. Then she turned away again and deliberately tipped her head toward one shoulder to bare her neck.

His rhythm stuttered as understanding dawned. "My sweet mate. That is the taste I crave more than any other. Soon. I promise."

She trembled at his words. He intended to bite her, to lay claim to her for the rest of their lives. She would have his mark on her body soon, and it would never fade.

Their lovemaking grew wilder, the pace more frenetic. She had to brace herself against his powerful thrusts as he filled her body again and again. His cock slid in and out, every stroke adding to her pleasure. She rocked back against him, changing the angle of their bodies and milking his shaft with her body until they were both mindless with pleasure.

Then, just as she was about to come undone, he stopped. Still buried hilt deep inside her, he curved his body over hers and wrapped a hand around her stomach before straightening up and taking her with him.

"Are you mine, Skye?" His voice was a rumble of sound near her ear.

"Yes, Yardan. I'm yours. Give me your mark so everyone will know it."

"With pleasure." He brushed his lips against the side of her neck, one hand still holding her to him while the other reached down to finger her clit even while he was still inside her.

"You are mine."

Then his teeth sank into her neck and her universe exploded into shards of crystalline bliss. Delicate, beautiful, and breathtaking.

She cried out, one hand clamping down on his wrist as the other cradled his head, holding him against her. She shuddered and arched as she came, riding his cock and his fingers as pure lust ignited in her veins.

He groaned against her throat, but she felt no pain, only intense pleasure where his fangs pierced her skin.

She came longer than she thought possible, and only then did he gently withdraw his fangs. He didn't let her go, though. He kept her kneeling in front of him, holding her up as he thrust into her until his cock twitched and thickened. He came inside her, jet after jet of his seed coating her womb.

When he was spent, they parted just long enough for them both to crawl onto the bed. They flopped down beside each other, breathless, flushed, and utterly spent.

After a few minutes she summoned the strength to roll onto her side so she could look at him. He lay on his back, eyes closed, his face as relaxed as she'd ever seen it.

"Hello, *mahoyen*," she murmured.

He turned his head and smiled at her. "Hello, my *mahaya*." Then he stretched his arms over his head and groaned contentedly. "It has been far, far too long since I've done that."

"How long?" She shouldn't ask him that question. What was in their past wasn't important.

"Since the day I took my vows. No distractions." He reached out and stroked her cheek with a gentle hand. "Not until you."

He rolled off the bed then, and she had a pang of concern that she'd said something wrong. Yardan didn't go far, though. He picked up his coat from the floor and rummaged through the pockets until he found what he was looking for. Then he held it up for her to see.

"We use this ointment to ensure that a claiming mark scars. Otherwise, the damn nanobots make it heal too perfectly." He pointed to her neck. "I want everyone to know you're claimed."

She laughed and patted the bed beside her. "I understand the sentiment. Make it permanent, my grumpy spymaster. Then we can talk about how I can go about marking *you*."

He rejoined her on the bed and then gestured to the *muhan* vine tattooed on his arm. "I'm already marked. This is the symbol of the *Naram T'kar*."

"You told me that mark represents your loyalty and devotion to your master." She winked at him. "I want something that marks you as *mine*."

15

———

Yardan paced around his office for the hundredth time today, walking right through projections of facts, figures, and faces that floated in the air everywhere he looked. He'd been moving things around in an attempt to reorganize the information... or his brain. He didn't care which, so long as it sparked an idea. No spark so far.

At least, not regarding the investigation. Skye was another matter. When it came to his mate, he had hundreds of ideas—all of them highly combustible.

He swatted at one of the projections even as he smiled, knowing Skye was across the hall, close enough he could catch the occasional trace of her scent.

He'd never imagined it possible to be happy and frustrated at the same time, but that's where he found himself.

The last few days had been a whirlwind of sex, laughter, discovery, and even more sex. The more he learned about Skye, the more he realized how well-suited they were. She had endured so much yet hadn't let it destroy the light in her soul.

She was stronger than he was and far, far kinder.

And that was part of his frustration. His mate was compassionate, loyal, and protective of every citizen of Haven. She was also one of the names he hadn't been able to strike from his list of suspects. His entire craft was based on the ability to read another being's character, and he was utterly certain she wasn't involved in the attack on the Vardarians. Unfortunately, his instincts alone weren't enough to remove her nor was the fact she was his *mahaya*. He had to be impartial. He had to find proof.

As one of the cyborgs working with the human colonists, Skye was in constant contact with the saboteur, Kara. By her own admission, she'd been near Kara's habi-pod several times during the period when the package of nanotech had been dropped off at Kara's cabin, and enough time had passed that the cyborgs' systems had automatically wiped any data that hadn't been deliberately archived. Even if it had been available to review, he couldn't eliminate the possibility that a spy wouldn't have been given the ability to manipulate their own files.

The cyborgs had been created by the corporate

cabal they called the Gray Men, and likely the same group was involved in this attack. That was another reason why the remaining spy had to be human or a cyborg. His species was new to this part of the galaxy. While Kade had been blackmailed into spying for a time, he'd drawn the line at handing over anything that would endanger Haven, and he hadn't even been a citizen at the time.

Yardan couldn't imagine what would push someone to turn against their entire species, especially since they'd be affected, too.

They'd interrogated Kara yesterday, though she'd been unable to add anything to the statements she'd already given. For him, it was a chance to read the expressions of the female who had brought so much suffering to the colony and his people. For Skye, it was a chance to confront the being who had deceived her and betrayed her trust.

It hadn't been enough for either of them, but it was all they'd get.

He'd started another investigation, too. One he hadn't told Skye about. Something about the Vardarian pilot who had flirted with Skye on their journey back from the platform still made his scales itch. It wasn't just his behavior toward Skye, though that still rankled. Something else was going on with that male, and he wanted to know what it was. Smuggling was his first guess. It was a common enough problem on every planet, and Bitan's daily runs back and forth between the colony and the orbital platform would give him ample opportunity. If he found proof of anything illegal, he'd report it to the leadership council. Maybe that would finally get them to create a legal system and a means to enforce it.

His thoughts chased themselves around his head like dust motes in a whirlwind, each one more annoying than the last.

Tyran was one of the most irritating of all. He'd met with the prince during one of the lulls in the sharhal. He'd left Skye to sleep and flown back to the palace to offer Tyran his resignation.

The prince refused to accept it. "You can't quit on me, Yardan. You're the only one on this whole planet qualified to finish this investigation. I am pleased you have found your *mahaya*, but your duty is not done. I'll have to go off-world to find a replacement. Until then, I need you to get back to work. You have a spy to find."

The fact the prince was right didn't make his decision to throw out centuries of tradition any easier to accept. It was rare for a spymaster to leave their station unless the one they reported to died and their successor chose to bring in someone else. Even that was rare, though it had happened to him when Tyran's father died and his sister had taken the throne. Even then, Yardan had retained his status within the small collective of beings who had earned the title.

This time would be different. This time, he'd

renounce his position and his status as a spymaster forever.

It went against all forms and traditions, but Yardan had agreed to stay on until a replacement could be found and introduced to his network, both here and off-world. All that he'd worked for would be handed over to someone else, and he'd have to figure out who he wanted to be going forward. Well, who he wanted to be, besides Skye's *mahoyen*. That was the one thing he was certain of.

Skye knew he was uncertain about his future, but each time it came up, she simply smiled, kissed him, and told him to stay focused on their current task—finding their spy.

As much turmoil as she'd brought to his life, it was all worth it. *She* was worth it.

They managed a few hours of work before the *sharhal* took hold again. Normally it would have lessened by now, but Skye's decision to delay the process had intensified things.

Not that he was complaining. It was the first time he hadn't spent every waking hour of his day working, and he refused to feel guilty about it. Mostly. But if the ancestors had wanted him to focus on his duties, they shouldn't have sent him a mate.

Tonight, he'd take Skye out in public for the first

time. He'd hoped to have a *harani* for her before that happened, but he'd wanted something special, and that took time. He'd contacted Damos and Tra'var one morning while Skye showered and told the two forge masters what he wanted. He hadn't bothered to swear them to secrecy. There was no point. According to his contacts, the entire colony was abuzz with the news that the spymaster had found his *mahaya*. Bitan must have started talking the second he left his *fraxxing* ship.

A sound at the top of the stairs snapped him out of his reverie. Skye appeared on the landing and for one brief, perfect moment, time stood still.

She descended the stairs like she was the empress herself, all elegance and grace. Her hair was gathered high on her head and held in place by some kind of sorcery known only to females, with just a few stray locks falling around her face.

Her outfit was styled in Vardarian fashion but with small changes that made it more a blend of both their cultures. The top was black with a rounded collar decorated with intricate needlework in greens and blues, but it had sleeves that came to her wrists and was made of a flowing fabric that fluttered softly as she moved. Her pants were made of the same material as the top, with matching needlework on the edge of the pant legs.

Seeing her like this made him want to abandon their plans to attend tonight's celebration and carry her back upstairs to her bedroom so he could unwrap her like a present and muss up her perfect hair.

He knew better than to try, though. Skye was looking forward to tonight, and he would not disappoint her. Instead, he held out his hand to her as she reached the bottom step. "You look even more beautiful than usual, my *ti'nar*."

"And you clean up very nicely yourself, my *mahoyen*." She touched the newly healed scar on the side of her neck. His mark. With a nod, he reached up to tap the mark she'd given him. At first she'd been reluctant to bite him hard enough to break the skin. To overcome her hesitation, he'd bitten her the next time they made love, and she'd marked him while lost in pleasure.

Tonight the entire colony would gather to celebrate the recovery of the Vardarians and to give recognition to their friends and neighbors who had kept the colony running and tended to the sick, even those who had resisted the idea of having the humans and cyborgs as part of their community. As one of the ones most resistant, it was important for him to be there.

Besides, it would give him a chance to observe and listen. Maybe he'd learn something useful.

The practice arena that had so recently served as an emergency shelter and hospital had been transformed yet again. The cots were gone, replaced with table after table of food and drink. The combination of scents was dizzying, reminding him of the markets and festivals of his youth.

He introduced Skye to a variety of Vardarian dishes, all of which he had the opportunity to experience with his full senses for the first time in years. She, in turn, encouraged him to try several human foods and even some prepared by the only Torski in the colony. Denz was a surprisingly talented cook, though he credited his many mothers and fathers with the recipes he used.

Both of them were the focus of a great deal of attention and a surprising number of congratulations that all seemed completely genuine. He did note that most beings approached him when he was with Skye, with only a few daring to speak to him when he was alone. That was fine by him. It allowed him to wander through the crowd without too much interference, listening to conversations and taking note of who stood together and which groups still kept apart.

He kept an eye on Skye, too. Not that was worried about her, but as his mate, she would always have some measure of his attention. Her happiness and safety were his top priorities now and forever more.

As he circulated around the arena, he tended to linger near groups of cyborgs and the few humans who had recently joined the colony. His suspect was most likely to be among them, and he needed to watch and listen in case someone gave away a key piece of information.

The only two beings he didn't see were Bitan and his *anrik*, Lavis. If they were staying away tonight, it would be because they didn't want to run afoul of a certain spymaster and his newly claimed *mahaya*, which proved they weren't complete fools.

He moved back to the tables laden with food, selecting a few new dishes at random as an excuse to linger near a group of cyborgs. They were all members of the recently formed rangers and included a number of beings who were not yet comfortable with their new, more civilized lifestyles. Axe was one of his top suspects, simply because there was almost no information on him. He lived outside the colony, staying in a cabin he'd built himself despite the fact it was the middle of winter. He'd also taken another new arrival under his proverbial wing—Cameron, a young human male they'd rescued from a mercenary ship sent to kidnap one of the human colonists. It was possible that one or both were spies of some kind.

He finished filling his plate without hearing or seeing anything useful and was about to move on when he sensed someone watching him. He raised his head and moved away from the table, using the motion to scan the crowd. Who was... *Qarf*.

Twenty meters away, Skye stood with one brow raised and her lips pressed into a thin line. His mate was not happy, and he wasn't sure why. He zipped back to the table, picked up something Skye had raved about and called a "brownie," and made his way over to her with the treat in his outstretched hand.

If what he'd heard was right, chocolate was his best course of action right now.

16

SKYE HADN'T ENJOYED an evening so much since the first parties she'd attended after the cyborgs had awoken on Liberty and discovered they were free. This party was even better, though, because the entire colony was here, and they were celebrating together. Not to mention she was here with Yardan, and he'd been warm, attentive, and more sociable than she'd ever seen him.

She'd only later noticed a pattern to his movements, and even then, it had taken her some time to realize what he was doing. He wasn't enjoying the party; he was *working*. That wasn't the real problem, though. It was who he was interested in. The Vardarians weren't the focus of his attention—only the cyborgs and humans. *Again.*

His bias was showing, and it infuriated her. She'd

thought they were past this issue, but apparently he wasn't ready to let go of his distrust of anyone different.

When he glanced up and saw her, she didn't bother hiding her feelings. She kept her gaze locked on his and waited, unmoving, while he hurried over to her with a brownie in hand.

A brownie was not going to fix this, but she was still slightly amused that he thought it might. *Slightly.*

"You and I need to have a word, Vin."

To his credit, he didn't argue. Instead, he broke the dessert in half, popped one piece in his mouth, and gave the other to her. She ate it on the way out.

He set aside his plate of food and followed her into the lobby of the arena. When he slowed, she kept moving. She had no intention of talking to him inside. Too many beings present would overhear, and she didn't want anyone listening to this conversation.

Her jacket was still inside, but her medi-bots immediately altered her metabolism to cope with the cold. Of course, that might have been anger keeping her warm, but either way, she was able to ignore the weather and focus on Yardan.

"This is a party, not an opportunity to gather intel," she said.

"In my line of work, everything is an opportunity. You know that."

She waved off his answer dismissively. "You deserve time off, too. But that's not the real problem. Your bias against non-Vardarians is affecting the investigation. We don't know who the spy is, and we certainly can't be sure it's not a Vardarian."

His jaw clenched and his brow creased into a scowl. "It can't be a Vardarian. Every Vardarian in the colony was infected with helix fever other than Damos, and we know why he wasn't affected. Who would put themselves at risk like that?"

She resisted the urge to roll her eyes at him. "The infection was an unexpected result of the experiment. Whoever it was didn't know what would happen. You can't eliminate every Vardarian as a suspect simply because they didn't know the real risk."

"While I appreciate your work and insight into this investigation, you are new to this type of work. I've been doing it longer than you have been alive."

"Did you..." she trailed off, too angry to express herself well.

"Remind you that I know more about this kind of work than you do? Yes. Tell me, Skye. How many humans and cyborgs aren't in attendance tonight?"

"Now you're testing me? I'm a cyborg, remember?" She played back the events of the evening currently recorded in her databanks and cross-referenced them with the list of every non-Vardarian on the planet. It only took a few seconds.

"They're all present. Which is more than can be said for your species. More than a dozen skipped the party. What does that prove?"

His expression softened for a moment as he searched for something to say. "A dozen?"

"Thirteen adults and three juveniles, not including the staff and guards still at the palace. I assume some of the parents stayed home with their offspring. You still haven't answered my question. What does that prove?"

He sighed. "I don't know."

"And did you learn anything tonight while you were spying on my people?"

Another sigh, this one edged with frustration and resentment. "No."

"Yet you stand there and tell me you know what you're doing. If I were you, I'd take some time to rethink your approach."

"About the investigation? Yes. Maybe I should."

He still didn't get it. "Not just the investigation, Yardan. Everything. Your bias is affecting everyone around you. Even me. You think a cyborg or a human did this. Does that mean you suspect me?"

His answer came too slowly, and she read the truth of it in the pinch of his brows and the way his gaze shifted before he spoke.

"I..." he started, and she cut him off before he could make things any worse.

"Don't lie to me. You *do* suspect me." Knowing that hurt more than she thought was possible, like a thousand chilled knives plunged into her chest and carved pieces out of her heart.

Hurting and humiliated, Skye left before he could

say anything else. Not even a Vardarian in flight was a match for a cyborg running at full speed. She didn't know where to go or what she'd do when she got there, but for the moment, she just needed to be alone.

In the end, she found herself back at the palace, pacing her office and stewing over the events of the night. To distract herself, she called up the latest information the computer had put together based on the information they'd received from the orbital platform. She hadn't had much time to look at it yet, and now seemed as good a time as any.

It took a bit for her to settle her mind enough to sit and really absorb the data, but once she did, she noticed something odd. She'd instructed the system to list all ships arriving from outside the system with all arrivals coming and going from the planet, looking for correlation points.

She found one.

A privately owned freighter called the *Tread Lightly* arrived regularly to deliver shipments of parts and equipment for the colony. At first glance, none of it was anything special, mostly agricultural including seeds, fertilizer, and machine parts. Only, it was the middle of winter, and these supplies were arriving every two weeks. The colony wasn't that large, and for now, most of the farming was being done by Vardarians using their own tech.

She looked again, and this time noted something else. The amount of goods arriving with each delivery was relatively small, which made sense considering the lack of demand but didn't explain why there were so many deliveries. Surely it would be more cost effective to send a larger ship with bigger cargo than to do all these smaller shipments?

Once the *Tread Lightly* had her attention, she noticed something else. Every time that ship arrived on the platform, the same cargo shuttle pilot from Haven was assigned to take delivery and bring the shipment planet-side. Given the number of ships Haven employed to make those runs, that seemed extremely unlikely. It might not be related to their current investigation, but something about it didn't sit right, so she kept investigating.

What she found had her on her feet and reaching for her comm unit.

"Hey, Phaedra. I need a favor."

Half an hour later, she was on her way back to the orbital platform aboard one of the prince's private ships. In exchange, Phaedra had wanted to know why she wasn't still at the party. Skye had promised to fill her in the moment she was airborne.

"He said *what?*" Phaedra's indignant reaction made Skye feel better about her own. Once she was alone, she'd started to second guess herself and the way she'd handled things with Yardan. While running away wasn't something she was proud of, it was nice to know she wasn't the only one angry at Yardan's approach to the investigation.

"He hasn't gotten over his distrust of anyone who isn't Vardarian. I think you're the only exception he's made."

"But you're his *fraxxing mahaya!*" Phaedra raged. "How could he possibly think you were involved? And the fact he actually admitted it is just... not even my males would be that foolish, and there are times..."

"Technically he didn't admit it. I just read his expression and knew."

"That isn't much of an improvement. I'm still going to give him shit the next time I clap eyes on him."

Skye laughed. "You do that. Just don't tell him where I am. I'm not ready to talk to him yet."

Phaedra's next words were gentle. "You okay?"

"I will be. I mean, it's not like we can undo the mating thing. We're stuck with each other, so we're going to have to figure out a way to get past this."

"You will. He's going to lose his mind when he can't find you. You know that. Right?"

"I know. But it's not like I'm leaving forever. I'm just popping up to the platform so I can check on a lead. Something that can't wait. I'll be back soon."

"You better be. I've seen a different side of Yardan these last few days. You're good for him, Skye, and I don't want to deal with the old version of him any longer than I have to."

"He's good for me too... when he's not making me furious." She could be her true self with Yardan—the version of her who wanted freedom but also enjoyed when someone else took charge and let her simply submit... but only to someone she trusted. Only to him.

She'd ended her call with Phaedra with a promise to check in later, and then the cockpit lapsed into silence.

She flew the ship herself. Like most cyborgs, the skills and knowledge she needed to fly just about anything had been programmed into her while she was still in her maturation tank. While Vardarian tech was different, it wasn't difficult to work out what she needed to know.

There were advantages to who and what she was, even if she didn't often think of it that way. They made her faster, stronger, healthier, and able to see patterns that purely organic brains might miss, like the one she'd found when she'd spent some time investigating the *Tread Lightly*. Not only was that ship meeting with the same colony pilot each time it docked, but it was always in the area when things went wrong on the planet. When Kade was blackmailed, when Maggie was abducted by mercenaries, and the damned ship was on approach for another delivery right now. It had to be involved somehow. If it was, the cargo pilot from Haven was their most likely suspect.

What the fraxx *has Bitan gotten himself into?*

According to the schedule, that idiot had skipped

tonight's party to make a run to the platform. The request looked legitimate, but when she dug into it, she couldn't find who had filed it or what ship the supposedly urgent delivery was supposed to be for. Later, she and Yardan would have to look into how that had been accomplished. It was starting to look like Bitan wasn't working alone.

Fraxx. She'd already filed a request to delay the departure of the freighter in case she didn't get there in time. Neither it nor Bitan's cargo shuttle had requested a departure time yet, but that could change at any moment.

She hadn't bothered to change clothes after leaving the party and she didn't own a firearm of any kind. All she had was the dagger Yardan had given her fastened to her belt and hidden beneath her long shirt. Between that and the skills she'd been programmed with, it would have to be enough. She might have been created to act as a nurturing den mother to the rest of her brethren, but she'd still received the same basic training as the rest of them. She was many things, but at her core, she was a soldier. Despite what Yardan thought about her abilities, she knew she was right about this.

Someone was threatening her home. It was her job to stop them.

17

———

Yardan stood outside the arena for longer than he cared to admit as he tried to figure out where he'd gone wrong and what to do next. He eventually gave up trying to figure out the first issue. It was no longer relevant. He'd clearly miscalculated and would have to apologize. He hadn't told Skye about her being on his suspect list because he didn't believe she could be involved, and her name was only there to try and show that he was being impartial.

Only... he hadn't been. Skye had made that point clearly. She'd accused him of being biased and failing to investigate things properly because he didn't believe his own people could be involved. He still believed that was likely true, but that didn't mean Skye was wrong. Could he have missed something because he'd been looking in the wrong direction?

He returned to the lobby to warm up, still

pondering matters. He tried to contact Skye, but her comm unit wouldn't connect him and only requested he leave a recorded message.

If the chocolate hadn't helped, he had no faith that a recorded apology would work any better. He needed to talk to her face to face.

He gathered up their coats and left without saying goodbye to anyone. He didn't want to explain what had happened, not even Tyran or his princess. *Especially* not the princess.

They'd ridden one of the autonomous vehicles to the party, but he didn't bother hailing one to take him home. Instead, he flew over the colony, circling Skye's home several times along the way. It was dark, but he couldn't tell if that meant she wasn't home, or if she'd gone to bed already.

Eventually he landed in the palace grounds. He briefly considered going back to his office but chose to go to his rooms instead. He'd change, make a mocha, and work from home.

He was halfway through his second mug when he decided to take a break from the main investigation while the system caught up with his new requests. He'd gone back to the beginning and kept his focus on the Vardarians this time, starting with the ones who had not attended tonight's event without a reason.

While he waited, he opened the other file waiting for his attention. The one pertaining to Bitan.

The male was definitely up to something. Unlike

most of the colony's cargo shuttle pilots, he often overnighted on the platform instead of returning home at the end of the shift. They all had to do it occasionally, but Bitan stayed so often he even had a room permanently assigned to him.

That was unusual, but hardly proof of criminality. Oddly, several complaints had also been filed by staff on board the platform about Bitan's behavior. Security had never been called, but Bitan had become verbally abusive on several occasions, and one maintenance worker stated he believed the pilot was impaired. That seemed odd, given that Vardarian nanotech scrubbed all intoxicants from its host's body too quickly to allow that kind of impairment. It shouldn't be possible for Bitan to have gotten so drunk as to become a problem for anyone, and his race had long ago stopped using narcotics since the effects would only last a few minutes at best.

Yardan stared off into space as he tried to piece everything together. Something was going on with that pilot, and he wanted to know what it was.

Before he could connect the dots, his computer chittered softly and sent yet another data file into the queue for review.

This one was for information he'd requested that afternoon as he tried once again to remove Skye from his list of suspects. For security reasons, he'd personally assigned several satellites to surveil the area where the humans had been confined until after they had completed their integration training. He'd kept that information to himself and had vowed not to even look at it unless there was a threat. The records had been sent to his personal server, where they'd sat unchecked and forgotten until today.

The computer had found something.

Yardan tapped the projection and the file opened, filling his living room with images that first relieved and then alarmed him.

He had the name of the spy now, but that knowledge didn't fill him with satisfaction at closing the case. He'd been right after all. The female in the images wasn't Skye, but it *was* a cyborg. Her name was Talia. He recognized her immediately because she'd been one of the first of her kind to find her *mahoyen* after coming to the colony. He knew both her mates well. They were honorable males, hardworking and honest. Why would she risk her mates' lives this way? It made no sense. Especially since his investigation had already revealed that Talia had never left the colony, not even for a short trip to the orbital platform.

Skye would be heartbroken when she learned about this. Talia was a friend and one of the cyborgs who had volunteered to help the newly arrived humans settle in. It was the perfect cover for a spy, and they'd all missed it.

"*Qarf.*" It wasn't the outcome he'd hoped for. Of all the cyborgs he'd considered, Talia had never even crossed his mind. By all appearances, she had embraced her new life and was deeply in love with her mates.

He stared at the footage that clearly showed her approach Kara's habi-pod to drop off the weapon that had stripped every Vardarian of their nanotech, almost dooming them all.

He'd been right all along, but even he had missed the threat living among them. If Talia was capable of doing this, who else might be working against them? How many cyborgs were involved?

He slammed a fist down on the arm of his chair and shot to his feet. He would arrest this cyborg and interrogate her until he got the answers he needed to keep the rest of the colony safe. Not just the colony but the prince, his consorts, and Skye.

He tried to reach her again, but her comm still refused to connect him. This time, he left a voicemail telling her he'd found a suspect and that she needed to get in touch quickly so he could update her. He'd give her a name once they could speak directly. This wasn't news he could drop on her in a message.

He was already out the door when the next problem occurred to him. The entire colony, including most of the palace guards, was at the party tonight. It would go on for hours yet, which meant very few were available to accompany him to make this arrest. He'd need at least six because no Vardarian male would meekly accept the arrest of their *mahaya*. Guilty or not, they would protect her, even though she was a cyborg and more than capable of protecting herself.

That realization was followed by another. The suspect and her mates were likely still at the party. Approaching them in a building packed with beings who were still recovering from the attack was fraught with risk to everyone present, including Prince Tyran. Even if she came quietly, there was every possibility that one or more groups might get involved. He knew too well that the only difference between a group and a mob was a small spark at the wrong time.

No. He couldn't risk it.

With a growl of frustration, he slowed his pace and activated a channel he rarely used. It was a direct link to Tyran's implant, allowing them to speak instantly so long as they were within range of each other.

"Your Highness, we have a problem," Yardan subvocalized, ensuring no one could overhear him as he passed through the mostly empty hallways.

"Report, Spymaster."

He summarized what he'd learned for the prince as succinctly as he could. "The current situation makes apprehension of the spy problematic. I don't believe we have any choice but to delay for a few hours."

"Agreed," Tyran said, but then an unexpected voice joined their conversation.

"You spied on the humans and cyborgs without telling anyone?" Phaedra somehow managed to convey her outrage despite the fact she was subvocalizing... on a channel she was not supposed to have access to.

"You're not authorized to be on this channel!" Yardan retorted.

"Please. I was a hacker a lot longer than I was a princess. I've got access to *every* channel if I want it. But that is not the point right now. If you think Skye was mad at you for what you said earlier tonight, wait until she hears about this!"

"What happened earlier?" Tyran asked.

Phaedra cut in again. "Your spymaster told his *mahaya* she was a suspect in his investigation. You know, the one she's helping him with."

Yardan winced. "I never said that."

"Uh huh." Phaedra's tone was as dry as a desert wind. "You just didn't disagree with her when she asked you. No wonder she left the planet."

His hands balled into fists and he jerked to a halt in the middle of the hallway. "She *what*?"

"*Fraxx*. I wasn't supposed to tell you. She's going to be mad that I did. But since that cat has already jumped out the airlock, here's the deal. Skye needed to clear her head, and she had a lead she wanted to check out on the orbital platform. I loaned her one of the palace shuttles."

"The platform? Who was piloting? When did she leave?"

"Yep, the plat. Oh, and she flew herself. I talked to her about forty minutes ago, so she should be arriving shortly." Phaedra went quiet for a moment and then added. "Veth. If you think the suspect is a cyborg at the party, who the hell is she chasing up there?"

"I don't know." A chill crept down his spine to twine icy fingers around his gut. "What did she say to you? Her exact words, Princess. This is important."

Phaedra's voice was calm and measured in a way he rarely heard. "She didn't say much. Just that she wanted to check out a lead and that it couldn't wait. I'm sorry, Yardan. That's all I know. I can give you the transponder code for the shuttle she took. That will let you see when and where she docks."

"Thank you." He forced his shoulders to relax. "Your Highness, I'd like to requisition one of the—"

Tyran cut him off. "Take my private craft. It's the fastest available. I'll contact the platform's commander and tell them to provide all the support you require. They can keep an eye out for Skye and make sure she is informed you need to speak to her immediately. The other matter will wait until morning. Go find your *mahaya* and make sure she's safe."

"I will. Thank you."

He broke into a run before he'd uttered the last two words. When he caught up to Skye, he'd apologize, kiss her, and then punish her in ways that would make her blush for days... and not necessarily in that order.

~

He barely had the ship in the air when his comms chimed with an incoming message from Skye. It was a prerecorded video, but he still felt a rush of relief as he transferred it to the main screen and watched it while he flew.

Skye's face appeared on the monitor, and the sight of her made his heart ache. He'd sworn to protect her, and then he'd let her believe she was a suspect in their own investigation. He'd broken his vow and betrayed her trust in ways he was only beginning to understand.

He'd been a stubborn, stars-forsaken fool.

"Hello, Spymaster." Skye winced, shook her head, and started again. "Hello, my *mahoyen*. You are as stubborn as a mogat and as prickly as that *muhan* vine you wear tattooed on your arm, but you are still my mate, and I know we'll find our way through this." A glimmer of a smile touched her lips. "Probably.

"I'm on the orbital platform. I found something connecting a freighter called the *Tread Lightly* with one of our shuttle pilots—the ones running cargo back and forth to the colony. I'm including the information so you can judge for yourself, but what you need to know is that both the *Tread Lightly* and our shuttle pilot are on the platform right now. It looks like a rendezvous."

Yardan swore and pushed the engines of the shuttle even faster.

"I'm going to talk to Bitan. He's the shuttle pilot I think is involved. Yes, *that* Bitan, the Vardarian who flew us back to the planet. If I speak to him alone, I think I can get him to tell me the truth about what's going on. He's a decent male, and I cannot imagine why he did what he did.

"I'm telling you this because I need you to deal with the *Tread Lightly* and make sure it doesn't leave before we can get the answers we need. You have the authority to make that happen. I don't."

Skye smiled, kissed her fingertips, and then pressed them to the screen. "We'll talk soon, but not until after I prove that honey works better than vinegar."

The moment the recording ended, he tried to contact her, but she didn't pick up. Of course she didn't. In her position he wouldn't have answered, either. She was angry, hurt, and determined to prove herself.

She also didn't know the danger she was in. Skye thought she was going to talk to a former lover about something she was certain he'd regret. Yardan feared it was more complicated than that.

The reports about his aggressive, abusive behavior painted a very different picture. Whoever Bitan had been once, when he was on the platform, he turned into someone else.

Frustrated and desperately worried about Skye, he broke every rule and tradition of his calling and reached out to the one male he truly trusted. "Prince Tyran. My friend, I need your help."

18

———

Sending Yardan a message telling him where she was and what she was doing was the right call. She hadn't been certain at the time, but the moment it was done, a weight fell from her shoulders.

She'd given the same advice to her fellow cyborgs more than once. Holding on to anger and hurt did the most damage to the one carrying that burden, even if it seemed easier to stay mad.

She'd already contacted Commander Sai on the orbital platform to explain why she was coming back and what she needed done. Apparently, the *Tread Lightly* was a privately owned freighter. It had an advanced AI installed, allowing it to function with only a single operator on board. That wasn't uncommon in smaller ships, and it meant she only had one person to worry about—an older human male named Chad Irons. He was currently on board his ship. Yardan would make sure that if the ship attempted to depart, it would meet with delays that should keep Irons frustrated but stuck until they were ready to deal with him.

Her comm was tucked into her pocket in silent mode to ensure she wasn't distracted at the wrong moment during her conversation with Bitan. Keshta knew where she was and had security on alert. Hopefully that wouldn't be necessary.

Bitan was a cocky, fun-loving male, but he wasn't violent or mentally unbalanced. Given their connection, she intended to appeal to the male she knew and try to get him to reach out for the help he so obviously needed. Whatever reason he had for acting against his home, they'd find a way out of it.

At least, that's what she hoped.

Keshta gave her access to the platform's surveillance systems and she quickly scanned through the most likely spots her quarry might be. He wasn't in any of the recreational areas or the entertainment section, but she did find footage of him entering a room in the residential sector. A quick search of the platform's database confirmed that he rented this space instead of using one of the communal rooms offered to other pilots staying overnight. Why would he do that?

There was only one way to find out.

She found the room and activated the chime

announcing her presence. No answer. She hit the chime again, waited a beat, and then spoke aloud. "Bitan, it's Skye."

This time she heard a groggy moan that slowly formed into a single word. "Skye?" A muffled thump followed and then another groan.

"You okay in there?" It sounded to her like she'd woken him from a dead sleep, but that didn't seem likely given he'd entered that room only a half hour before she'd arrived.

"S'okay. Just got a little dizzy stan-standing up."

His words were slurred and he claimed to be dizzy. That sounded less like he was sleepy and more like he was intoxicated, but his nanotech made that impossible. Something didn't add up here.

Another thump shook the outer wall followed by a string of mostly incoherent cursing not even her improved hearing could decipher. Then the door opened to reveal a disheveled form peering at her from slitted, bloodshot eyes.

"Why aren't you at the party?" Bitan asked, each word carefully pronounced to avoid slurring this time.

"I was, but something came up and I volunteered to make the trip here so the others could stay and enjoy themselves."

She paused at the doorway as she registered every detail she could make out in the dimly lit room visible beyond Bitan. Rumpled blankets were strewn on the bunk set against the back wall and the place looked like it hadn't been visited by a house-cleaning bot in a while. A plate of partially congealed *something* that might have been the leftovers of a meal or the beginnings of a new lifeform sat on a small fold-out table.

Bitan leaned into the doorway, casting his eyes up and down the empty hall. "You didn't bring *him*?"

She shrugged and decided to go with the truth. "We had a fight. I figured a little alone time would be good for us both."

"Still can't believe you're mated to the sshpymaster." Bitan made the last word sound like a curse, albeit one that came with a spray of spittle.

"It was a surprise to us all." She smiled at her former lover and cocked her head to one side. "Are you okay? I noticed you weren't at the party tonight and you don't seem yourself right now." She scanned him as they chatted, and nothing she saw made her happy. His heart rate was too slow, and so was his breathing. His pupils were little more than pinpricks and his silver skin looked dull. He *was* intoxicated, but by what?

Bitan grinned a little too broadly and leaned in closer. "I'm not myself. I'm better Bitan. And every time I get more of this stuff, I get better still." His eyes widened and one hand lifted to cover his mouth. "Not supposed to talk about that."

"You can talk to me. We're friends. Right?"

He leered at her, something dark shadowing his features and making her uneasy. His next words came out in his native tongue. "We were more than *friends*. And I can't talk to you about this because you're with *him* now." The slur shifted to more of a sibilant hiss when he changed languages.

She was so focused on Bitan she almost missed the new sound just at the edge of her hearing. Footsteps, and they were getting louder.

"Someone's coming. Why don't we go inside and talk?"

Instead of letting her in, Bitan went wide-eyed with sudden panic. "Someone? Who? Time? Did I lose track of the time?"

He jerked around like a marionette with tangled strings, some of his movements exaggerated while others were cut short.

"What's wrong?" she asked, sharpening her tone to try and reach the clearly panicked male.

Bitan went still and stared at her. "It's *him*," he hissed, still speaking Vardarian. "You don't want to meet him. I don't want you to meet him. Go!" Bitan made a shooing motion and retreated into his room. The door closed before she could ask anything else, and the footsteps kept getting closer.

She turned and headed away from whoever was approaching, trying to be quick without looking suspicious or creating too much noise. If whoever Bitan was afraid of heard her running off, it wouldn't go well for any of them.

A servo-droid rolled out of a hatch on the inner bulkhead, and she hurried over to that section. Where there was one droid there should be more, and they'd be stored... She spotted a slightly inset panel and pressed her hand to it. The cover slid back, revealing a simple access pad. Whoever had used it last had left smudges on the keys, and it only took her a few tries to figure out the order of the numbers.

She ducked out of sight, taking an extra second to look back down the corridor toward Bitan's door.

She only got a brief glimpse, but it was enough to show her that the new arrival was a human male of average height and weight with bland features and medium brown hair. She'd seen a picture of the *Tread Lightly*'s operator, Irons. This wasn't him.

So, who the fraxx was he?

The unknown male stopped at the door she'd just left, which proved that Bitan's fearful reaction had a real cause.

Then the door to her hiding place slid shut, sealing her in with the droids and various maintenance supplies. The only light came from the charging ports for the servo-droids, making the area around her feet light up like a constellation of orange and blue stars.

She pressed her ear to the door and listened intently. She needed to hear their conversation.

Bitan's greeting was strained and brief. His visitor

told him to get back inside in a harsh tone that made Bitan's next words come out at a higher than usual pitch as he invited the visitor into his room.

Fraxx. Once the door closed, she couldn't make out what was being said, but her hearing was good enough to ensure she caught the tone, if not the form of the words being exchanged.

Bitan rarely spoke, and when he did, all she heard was anxious pleading. The newcomer did most of the talking, his voice ranging from dismissive to furious. She caught a few words each time his voice rose, including terms like failure and useless.

Her comm unit vibrated several times while she eavesdropped, but she had to keep her focus on the conversation for now. Whoever it was and whatever they needed to say would have to wait.

After five minutes of heated discussion, things eventually calmed down. Bitan's tone changed to one of grateful, almost pathetic relief, and his visitor stopped his tirade, his last words spoken softly and without rancor.

Whatever was going on, the worst of it must be over. She'd been on the verge of intervening for Bitan's sake, even though doing so might have put both of them in danger.

What the *fraxx* had the fool gotten himself involved in? Once this asshole was gone, she needed to speak to Bitan again, and she wouldn't leave until he told her everything.

She had her hand raised to open the door to the maintenance room when a familiar voice shouted inside her head.

"Skye! For the love of gravity, answer me!"

She winced and put a hand over her ear, which was a completely useless gesture because her friend River was on an internal channel the cyborgs used. The channel had a range limitation that shouldn't have allowed contact given the distance between the platform and the colony below. *"Why are you calling me, River? Where are you and what's wrong?"*

"What's wrong? Your mahoyen *has lost his mind. That's what's wrong. Something about his reckless mate going off to investigate a spy on her own with no backup. I have heard far too much about what he's going to do to you when he catches up to ever be able to look you in the eyes again. Spanking? I had no idea you were into that sort of thing."*

She couldn't stop a flush of heat creeping up her cheeks. *"He said* what? *I'm going to kill him."* Then the rest of what River said sank in. *"You're with Yardan? Where are you? What's going on?"*

"If you ever checked your comms, you'd know what was going on." Some of the worry in River's voice had been replaced by gentle reproof. River had been created to fulfill the same niche as Skye and Talia. Empathy and caring were hard-coded into their genetic makeup.

River continued. *"Yardan has tried to reach you*

ever since he got your message. When you didn't respond he borrowed the prince's shuttle and went after you. Then he got your recorded message and now me, Tyran, Braxon, and Edge are on our way to you. What are you doing up there?"

"I'm doing my job. And he should be more worried about planning a really impressive apology when we next meet. If he thinks having witnesses will save him, he's mistaken."

"I don't know what you mean about an apology. Honestly, I don't know much about what's going on other than he thinks you may be in danger. Tyran said something about there being a cyborg spy in the colony."

Skye smacked her open palm against her thigh and swore. "He's still looking in the wrong place. The spy isn't a cyborg. At least, I don't think so. It's a Vardarian pilot I know. I saw him and... well, I don't know how it's possible, but he was out of his mind on some kind of pharma when I saw him. Then someone else showed up and my friend panicked and told me to hide. The two males argued. Now the other male is gone and I need to go check on my friend. There's no danger."

She paused and then added. "Tell Yardan I'm not the one he should be worried about."

"Done. Considering his response, should I schedule the two of you for relationship counseling once this is over?" River asked, her tone mildly amused but still mostly worried.

"We'll figure it out. Besides, no one in the colony is certified for that kind of thing."

"For you, I'd take a crash course."

Skye took a moment to imagine what Yardan's reaction would be if someone else tried to make suggestions about how to improve their relationship. It got ugly quickly, so she relinquished the idea with a smirk.

"I don't think that will be necessary. I'll see you when you get here."

"Stay safe." River signed off and the inside of Skye's head was quiet once more. She hadn't realized how quiet until now. She'd never been out of range of her entire group before, but she'd been too focused on other things to notice. Now she had, it felt odd and more than a little lonely.

Maybe once she and Yardan got things figured out, she'd ask if he wanted a comm link between them. There was a way to make that work, several of the other cyborgs already had that link with their Vardarian mates. It would be nice to have that connection with him.

She slipped out of her hiding place and retraced her steps to Bitan's door. When she activated the chime this time, she heard no reaction. She hit it again and then again, but Bitan didn't stir.

Concerned, she pressed her ear to the door. From this close she should be able to hear him breathe if she focused, but the silence stretched on.

Fraxx.

She pulled her comm out and made an urgent call to Commander Sai. "It's me. I've got a potential emergency here. I need you to override the lock on a private room? Sector six, level fourteen, door two-one-seven."

Keshta didn't ask any questions, and a few seconds later the door slid open. "Thank you. Stay on the line and I'll let you know what I... *veth*."

Now she knew why she hadn't heard Bitan breathing. He'd already drawn his last breath.

She scanned him but found no signs of life. His body sprawled across his bunk, one leg hanging off the side. His eyes stared at nothing, and the smells of death already lingered in the air. Skye swallowed hard against both the nausea and grief that tried to choke her.

The only thing she could do for Bitan now was to catch the man who'd killed him.

"Skye?" Keshta spoke, startling her.

"I'm here. There's been a murder. Send someone to guard the door and don't let anyone in until the prince or the spymaster give the all clear. And I need you to double check on the *Tread Lightly* and confirm no one left the ship."

"A murder?" The shock in the commander's voice echoed Skye's own feelings. Haven had been violated again.

"I can confirm that no one has left the ship we have under surveillance. No change."

Skye scowled. That didn't make sense. If Bitan's killer wasn't from the *Tread Lightly*, where the hell did he come from?

She backed out of the room, turned sharply and then took off at a run in the only direction her suspect could have gone.

She wanted answers, and Bitan needed justice.

19

Nothing tonight had gone according to plan. First, he'd fought with Skye. Then she'd left the planet in order to chase down a lead without him. Now he was on his way to the orbital platform, but he wasn't alone. When he'd asked Tyran for help, he had expected the prince to enable him to mobilize any resources he might need and make sure Commander Sai complied with any requests. Instead, the prince, his *anrik*, and two members of the leadership council who had happened to be nearby when he'd contacted Tyran were all onboard another ship speeding toward the platform. Tyran had been updating them about the situation with Talia at the time, and they'd insisted on coming.

Yardan had done his best to persuade the entire group to stay on Liberty, but the prince had pulled rank, and now he had a four-person party determined to join him in this late-night adventure. When had his life gotten this *qarfing* complicated?

The answer was easy. It happened the moment Skye had informed him she was his *mahaya*. Since then, nothing had been simple. He got the feeling it never would be again.

The docking clamps hadn't even finished locking down the ship before he was up and headed for the door. Because this was the prince's personal vessel, they had a small armory on board. He was now armed with a fully charged blaster along with the blade he always carried.

His comm chirped before he'd taken more than three steps onto the platform, and he grunted in frustration, slowing down so he could fish it out of his pocket and see who was trying to reach him.

Skye.

"Where are you?" he demanded in a voice even he knew was too brusque for the moment.

"I'm tracking down the human male who killed Bitan. At least, that's what I think happened."

That drew him up short and he had to shove aside the wave of concern for Skye that threatened to overwhelm him. "Bitan is dead? River said you just spoke with him a little while ago. Are you hurt? What happened?"

"I wasn't there when it happened. I was hiding." He caught the faint note of guilt in her tone and made a note to address that at some future time.

"As for what happened, I'm not sure. All I know is Bitan was afraid of someone, and then that someone showed up. They argued, and I thought everything had calmed down. The male left and I went to check on Bitan. He was dead, and now I'm trying to find the son of a starbeast who killed him. I heard him coming and I know which way he went when he departed, but now it's like he's vanished. None of the cameras have caught a glimpse of him."

Her comment made his scales tighten. He'd read something about a similar case...

"Don't rely on visuals. Scan for heat signatures and other anomalies. He might be using a personal shield generator."

"Got it. What the fraxx is a personal shield generator?"

"Corporation tech. Experimental as far as I recall, but it works to bounce or bend light so the one wearing it is more or less invisible. It's short term only, though. He can't keep using it for long."

"Which explains why he was visible when he approached Bitan's door. I got a look at him. Sending you the image now."

A second later he was looking at the most mundane human he'd ever seen. Everything about him was unremarkable, right down to the unadorned gray ship-suit he wore."

"You've forwarded this to station security?"

Skye sounded annoyed. "Of course. I might not

have years of training like you, but you could give me some credit."

He snorted. "You went off planet alone to follow up on a lead. Alone. Did I mention that part?"

He half expected her to argue. She didn't. "You have a point. And I am sorry about that. I thought I'd be talking to a friend to help him find a way out of a mess he'd gotten into. This is..."

"More than either of us expected," he finished for her. "We'll discuss your punishment later. Right now, I need your position."

Instead of telling him, a map of the platform appeared in one corner of his screen. It had two icons, one marked as his, the other Skye's. She was three levels below him and two sectors over, but as he watched, her icon moved. He could track her in real time. "Now that is a handy skill. I'm on my way. If you find the suspect, do not engage."

Skye laughed. "No problem. I didn't bring a firearm. If it comes to a fight, I'll be doing it with that lovely dagger you gave me."

"In that case, really, *really* do not engage. You are more important than any investigation, my *mahaya*. Be careful."

She blew him a kiss and disconnected, leaving just the map and the icons.

He broke into a run, determined to catch up to Skye before she caught up to their suspect.

He almost made it.

Tyran and the others managed to dock closer to Skye than he had and were on their way to rendezvous with everyone from the other direction. Edge and River used their heat detection and other scanning functions to ensure the suspect hadn't slipped past them, which meant they now had him surrounded.

He rounded the curved outer ring of the platform and finally set eyes on Skye, but the rush of relief at seeing her alive and well was short lived.

She was alone in the corridor, still dressed in the same stunning outfit she'd worn to the party. Had that really been only a few hours ago?

He scanned the corridor but couldn't see anything out of place. As far as he could tell, no threat was present.

He was wrong.

The voice of an unseen human male spoke a line of gibberish that his translator couldn't parse, and Skye collapsed to the deck.

A switch flipped inside Yardan and his training took over. He loosed a battle cry that held as much grief as fury as he charged forward, his blaster filling the air with sizzling bolts as he tried to locate his invisible adversary.

He refused to look down at Skye, afraid he'd see some proof that she was already dead. He didn't know her status, and he clung to the belief that whatever had happened to her wasn't fatal. He didn't understand what could be wrong. He'd heard words, not weapons fire. What harm could words do to someone as strong as Skye?

One of his shots slammed into empty air and impacted with a flurry of sparks. He snapped out two more shots in quick succession, never slowing his pace. One flew past the area, but the other struck something, and this time the air shimmered and then fractured like thin ice shattering beneath a hammer blow. Now he could see the suspect, the same bland-faced male from the image Skye had sent.

Yardan spread his wings and roared as he closed the final distance between them.

To his shock, the other man turned and fled.

"I don't think so," he muttered as he drove himself forward and then pushed off, using his wings to lift and carry him forward so he tackled the suspect from behind.

They went down in a tangle, but again Yardan's opponent surprised him. The male didn't struggle at all. He went limp and dropped to the deck, the two of them rolling over several times before finally coming to rest with Yardan looming over the suspect with his forearm pressed to the other male's throat.

"What did you do to her?" It wasn't the question he should be asking this male, but it was the one that mattered most.

Blood smeared the human's chin and coated his lips in crimson. He'd split his lip when he'd hit the floor, and when he shot Yardan a cruel smile, it only deepened the cut. "I reminded her that freedom is an illusion for her kind."

"Will she live?" he demanded.

The man's lip curled into a sneer. "It will continue to exist, yes. But don't fool yourself, that is a piece of machinery, not a living being. We created them, and we will reclaim our property eventually. It would be best if you didn't get too *attached*. Not to the cyborg or anything in this part of the galaxy. Your kind need to go back where you came from."

There was no mistaking the loathing in his eyes as the suspect spewed his venomous words. Kara had recited the same kind of hate-filled nonsense when she'd tried to justify what she'd done. It sickened him to hear it, but it also made it clear who they were dealing with.

"I thought Nova Force hunted you all down already. How many Grays are left?"

The male laughed. "You can't kill a shadow. You'll learn that soon enough."

"I can kill you right now. Give me one reason why I shouldn't."

"That's easy. You can't kill me, Spymaster. I'm already dead."

The body beneath him went limp and the light went out of the suspect's eyes.

"What? No!" Yardan shook the male and then took his pulse in all the spots a human's heartbeat was easily felt.

Nothing. The male was dead, and he had no idea how. Dammit, he hadn't even gotten a name.

Footsteps clattered down the corridor and he looked up to see Tyran and the rest of his party running toward them. Yardan scrambled to his feet and gestured to the body. "He's dead, but secure him in case he doesn't stay that way. I need to check on Skye."

He managed to make his voice sound gruff and level, but inside he was ready to scream. Had the nameless bastard told him the truth, or had he lost his mate before they'd even gotten started?

He dropped to his knees beside Skye's still form and touched her shoulder with a shaking hand. As slowly and gently as he could, he turned her onto her side. A quick check confirmed that she was still breathing, and some of the knots in his stomach untied themselves.

He ran his hands down her front and back to look for injuries but found nothing. He couldn't even tell why she'd collapsed, though it was hard to think past the adrenaline still coursing through his system.

"Skye. Come back to me." He touched her cheek but got no reaction. Her breathing was regular, and when he checked it, her pulse was soft but steady.

Once he accepted she wasn't going to wake yet, he gathered her into his arms and picked her up off the floor. He had to get her to a med-bay. They'd know what to do. He hadn't been fast enough to prevent her from being hurt, but he'd taken down her attacker and now he'd make sure she was taken care of.

He was so focused on Skye it took him longer than it should have to register what was happening ahead of him. Edge was shouting and pointing at the dead body, and River nodded back in confirmation of... something. Before Yardan could make sense any of things, Edge grabbed the prince and tossed him over his shoulder while River did the same with Braxon. Then the two cyborgs ran toward him.

"Bomb!" Edge yelled. "Go. Go. Go."

Yardan spun and sprinted away. Despite his speed, both cyborgs quickly caught up. Instead of leaving him behind, they somehow linked hands and swept him along with them, their arms pressed hard into the small of his back.

Tyran barked orders despite the fact he was draped awkwardly over Edge's shoulder and upside-down.

Yardan couldn't hear every word in the chaos, but he heard enough to know the prince was warning someone about the bomb and ordering the blast doors closed.

Warning lights strobed and the piercing screech of emergency sirens sounded as the station went to full alert.

The heavy doors were already moving when they reached them, but the three of them surged past in a desperate sprint to safety. Every second he expected the bomb to go off and end their mad race, but they cleared the doors without being blasted to ash or being sucked out into space.

The cyborgs slowed first, and River caught his arm to help him slow down and stay on his feet once they were no longer pulling him along.

The three of them turned to stare at the blast doors, all of them tensed in anticipation of an explosion.

Nothing happened.

After a few more seconds of nothing, Edge set Tyran back on his feet, and then River did the same for Braxon.

He held tightly to Skye. She hadn't stirred or reacted at all during their headlong run. Her face was slack and her body hung limply in his arms. He shouldn't be standing here, waiting to see if anything else went wrong. If he lost her... No. He couldn't even think about it. He needed to get her to a med-bay.

He needed her to live.

"Skye collapsed. I don't know what's wrong with her but she needs help," he stated to the others.

"Injuries?" River asked.

"None I can see. He said something to her. My translator couldn't make it out. Then she was down and she's nonresponsive."

Both cyborgs looked at each other, their eyes wide with concern.

"What? What do you think it was?" he demanded. Worry sharpened his words to spear points.

"Those bastards," Edge muttered.

River turned to look at Skye, her expression full of horror. "More codes? But how? We had those scrubbed once we arrived here at the colony."

Yardan opened his mouth to insist they explain, but his words were lost in a deafening explosion that made the deck shudder beneath them and sent a shock wave tearing through the platform.

He cradled Skye against his chest and fought to stay on his feet. If they both survived this, she was never leaving his sight ever again.

20

Skye came back to herself all at once. It wasn't a comfortable sensation. One moment she wasn't aware at all, but the next she was almost overwhelmed with information as everything came back online within a few nanoseconds.

She'd experienced full system reboots before, but that had been when she was a prisoner, which she wasn't anymore.

Or was she? Oh fraxx. Had she been captured again?

She sprang to her feet, fists clenched and ready to fight.

"Easy, Skye. You're safe."

She turned toward the voice. Yardan sat on a stool beside the bed she must have been lying on when she woke up. His hands were raised in a pacifying gesture, his expression one of utter relief. "You came back to me."

She dropped her fists and fell into his arms. "Of course I did. We've got unfinished business."

He chuckled and wrapped her in a hug so tender she almost melted away.

"A whole lifetime of it."

They stayed like that for a long time, soaking in the warmth and presence of the other until she felt grounded and content again.

"What happened?" she asked as she raised her head to look at him.

"That's what I want to know. What do you remember?"

She thought back and then shuddered. "He reset me. Used a code I've never heard before. That shouldn't have been possible. Hey, what happened to him?"

"He used a reset code on you, yes. That's what we all think happened. As for the suspect, he's dead. An implanted explosive device. No one was hurt and that part of the platform can be repaired.

"Fortunately, we have a Nova Force agent in residence right now, and she is taking care of that part of the investigation. I had somewhere else I needed to be."

He uttered a low growl and nuzzled the side of her jaw with his lips. "You were reckless, my *mahaya*. I told you not to engage the suspect."

"He was hiding behind a support strut. I didn't realize he was there until he moved."

"Hmm." Yardan didn't sound convinced. "Are you telling me you'd like me to consider that when I determine your punishment?"

Despite everything, a small thrill of desire zinged through her at his words. "Punishment? I caught a spy that you missed because you were convinced it couldn't be a Vardarian."

"Yes, you did. And then you decided to interrogate that suspect alone, even knowing his contact was likely on the station." He kissed her softly. "Reckless."

"And you were stubborn. Now do you believe a cyborg wasn't the spy?" She'd meant to tease him, but her mate's expression darkened.

"I wish I could agree with you, but I know differently. We had more than one spy in our midst."

"How many?" Part of her didn't want to know. *Veth*, that part didn't want to talk about any of this right now.

"Four." He sighed and then lifted his head to look into her eyes. "Bitan was the only one who knew what he was doing. The others..."

That made no sense. How could someone betray the colony without knowing what they were... oh.

Oh *fraxx*. No.

"Who was the cyborg you can prove was involved?" she asked, not ready to deal with her suspicions head on.

"Talia. She brought the nano-swarm to Kara. I talked to her over a vid-link while you were out. She has no memory of doing it." He sighed again. "I believe her."

"Who else?"

"River. Not that we have any way of knowing what she may have done, but so far, only three cyborgs we've found were programmed with a second set of override codes. Edge is calling them sleeper codes."

She tried to pull out of his arms as what he told her sank in, but he wouldn't let her go. "Talia. River. And me. I'm the third spy?"

"Not so much a spy as a sleeper agent. One completely unaware of their status. At least that's the theory right now. It's only been a few hours and we are going to have a lot of work to do to sort all this out. We've deactivated every code we could find, but you're going to need to be scanned several more times to be sure."

"And so is every other cyborg in the colony. You were right. I *was* a suspect."

"I was wrong about so many things. I should have told you what I was doing and why I couldn't remove you from the list even though I knew you'd never betray your home. I am sorry, my *mahaya*. You deserved better. But I warned you of that the day you claimed I was your *mahoyen*."

She snorted. "Don't be an idiot. I don't care what you think I deserve. I *want* you. Even if you are a stubborn, thorny pain in the ass. You are mine, and that's that."

He stared at her for a long time and then smiled softly and stroked her cheek. "I will love you until my last breath rejoins the eternal wind. You are mine. Always."

"Even now that you know I was well... compromised? I might have done terrible things, and I will never even know about it."

"You haven't done anything. If you were ever activated, there's no sign of it. Even if they did use you, it wasn't your choice. They took that from you and the other females. They stole your choices from you *again*. They will come to regret that mistake."

"Yes, they will." She didn't know how, but Yardan was right. She was tired of being used by the Gray Men, or whoever was behind all of this. It had to be the Grays, though. They were the only ones who could have known about the secret codes implanted in her software.

She had so many questions, but she didn't need to start hunting for answers right away. The most important thing she needed to do right now was to embrace her new life.

"How long do I have to stay here?" she asked, gesturing around them. She knew where she was now, in a medical cubby. By the size she assumed they were still on the platform.

"Now that you're awake, you need to be cleared by a healer. Once that's done, I'm taking you home."

"But what about the investigation? We have a lot of work to do to wrap that up." She wasn't just asking about the case. She was trying to work out if she still had a part to play.

"We'll get to that. But first you and I are going home. Together." He kissed her again and this time his touch wasn't so gentle. "Then I am going to make you understand the consequences of recklessness. It may take us hours for the lesson to sink in." He nipped her lip and ran a possessive hand down her back to cup her ass. "I intend to be very thorough."

To her surprise the prince and the others in his party were all nearby. None of them had wanted to leave until they were sure she was okay. River did her best to hide it, but Skye could tell her friend was as unsettled as she was over the revelation that they had been infected with the sleeper codes.

They all exchanged hugs and greetings, but River hugged her tighter and longer than anyone else.

"We'll get through this," Skye said over their link.

River just nodded slightly, but her eyes were full of doubt.

The moment River moved away Edge stepped in beside her. He didn't touch River or say a word, but

Skye got the sense he was trying to comfort her. He just didn't know how.

She briefly considered giving him a few hints but then decided against it. The two of them needed to figure this out on their own, just like she and Yardan had.

To bring back all three of the ships required some reorganization. Tyran and Braxon took the prince's personal shuttle, and Edge and River took one, leaving her and Yardan to fly down in the other.

Once they were underway, both of them uttered a sigh of relief at almost the exact same moment. They looked at each other and laughed.

"Happy to be heading home?" she asked.

"Happy to be going home with you." Yardan reached out and took her hand. "When I saw you go down..."

She couldn't imagine what that had been like for him. What would she have done in his place?

Probably the same thing he had. Flown into a rage and gone after the one who had hurt the being she loved.

Loved.

The word struck a chord deep in her soul. She loved him, and she needed to tell him so.

The second they were clear of the station she undid her safety harness and got to her feet.

Yardan glanced up at her curiously, but before he

could ask where she was going, she made it clear she wasn't going anywhere.

She toed off her boots and shimmied her way out of her pants, letting them fall to her feet before she stepped out of them.

"What are you doing?"

She grinned at him. "What does it look like I'm doing? The question is, are you going to join me?"

"Qarf, female. Here? Now?"

"Right here. Right now. I have something important to say and I want your complete attention." She skinned her top over her head, momentarily obscuring her vision.

When she could see again, her view had improved. Yardan had his shirt off and was trying to get out of his pants without leaving his chair.

"Leave that to me." She bent down and placed her hands over his to still them. Once he stopped moving, she slowly traced her fingers over the still-covered bulge between his legs.

His cock twitched at her touch, tenting the fabric even tighter. She kept teasing him until he uttered a low groan and rocked his hips up, grinding his length against her hand.

Feeling empowered, she worked his cock with one hand while she unfastened his pants with the other.

Once his cock was free, she spun his chair around to face her and then knelt between his feet.

Yardan placed his hand on her head but didn't try

to move her. He simply watched her, his gaze predatory and heated.

She bent over until the crown of his cock was against her lips and then let her tongue slip out from between her lips to swipe over the broad tip.

Her lover tensed, the arm of the chair beneath his hand creaking in protest at the pressure of his grip, though his touch on her head stayed gentle.

She pumped her fingers around the base of his shaft as her tongue glided over the crown, teasing him with light licks and slow strokes.

His thighs were taut and his breathing had a ragged edge to it by the time she finally took him deep into her mouth. He shouted in surprise and pleasure as most of his length slid past her lips. When she hollowed her cheeks to suck on him, his hips snapped up, pushing himself deeper.

She bobbed over his cock using hard, fast motions as her fingers caressed his root.

Just seeing him like this had her pussy wet with need, but she was loath to stop because she didn't want the moment to end. She had this male completely in her power, and it made every second even more intense.

She lowered one hand between her legs, working her fingers over her clit as she continued to pleasure him until her hips were jerking, and she was shuddering as she brought them both to the edge of orgasm.

"No. Your pleasure is *mine*," Yardan stated so suddenly she jerked her head up in surprise.

He caught her by her upper arms and drew her up off the floor. She let him pull her down onto the chair on top of him, straddling his thighs and gripping his shoulders for balance.

He didn't wait for her to get settled. Instead he slapped one hand firmly on her ass and fisted his cock with the other. He guided her over the head of his cock and then drew her down until he was pressed against her entrance.

Then he stopped.

"You now have my complete attention. What did you want to tell me?"

"What?" She had to struggle for a moment to remember the plan. "Oh, yes."

She wiggled her hips playfully as she leaned in so they were eye to eye, their mouths almost touching. "I love you, Yardan. And I will love you until my last breath."

He kissed her softly. "And then we will find each other again in the eternal wind."

After that, they had no need for words. They came together slowly, his cock filling every aching inch of her channel as her inner walls pulsed around him.

Their kisses were hot and hungry, blazing with a ferocity that seared her down to her soul. She rode him hard, rolling her hips and taking what she needed as she gave him everything she had—heart, body, and soul. Every touch held the promise of a lifetime of passion, and every kiss was a vow to love and protect each other as best they could.

They made love slowly and with an intensity so exquisite it was almost painful. The *sharhal* was no longer a raging inferno in their blood. It had changed into something else, something more subtle but far more focused.

It was like being in the heart of a star, or a white-hot forge, brilliant and beautiful. She could almost feel their bond growing stronger, as if the two of them were being forged into something new.

Overcome with emotion and need, she kissed him hard, and he groaned into her mouth. His grip on her hips tightened and he lifted her into the air, giving him enough clearance to power into her again and again.

Their movements became frenzied. Tangled tongues, bruising kisses, and the constant give and take as their bodies blended into one point of pure pleasure.

Yardan tore his mouth from hers and she knew what he needed. What they both needed. She tipped her head to one side, offering him the spot on her neck where he'd marked her.

When his fangs broke the skin, she cried out in pleasure, an orgasm tearing through her like a comet strike. She bit him back, and his cock swelled and jerked inside her.

They came together, shuddering and gasping as they chased the last notes of pleasure.

He settled her back down on the chair and she slumped over him, skin to skin. Her head rested in the crook of his shoulder, and she gently kissed the spot where she'd bitten him.

"Mine," she muttered contentedly.

"Yes, I am, and you are my *ti'nar dani*." His voice was a satisfied rumble.

She snuggled in with a happy sigh and then laughed when he added.

"But you are still going to be punished for your recklessness." He slapped her ass lightly and then nuzzled her hair. "I promise you will enjoy it almost as much as I do."

EPILOGUE

It was time.

Working together, he and Skye had completed the investigation. They knew who had brought the experimental nano-swarm to the colony and how it had been delivered. They also had confirmation that the Gray Men were involved. When platform security had boarded the *Tread Lightly*, they'd discovered it was abandoned and missing an escape pod, though they had no idea when Irons had slipped away. The ship's computer had been scrubbed of everything other than its current voyage, and not even Phaedra had been able to trace the vessel's real owners through the tangle of shell companies and asset transfers on record.

After the healers had done their tests, Bitan's remains had been claimed by his *anrik*. In shock at the sudden death of his friend and blood-brother, Lavis would soon be leaving Liberty to take Bitan's body home to his family. No one knew when, or if, Lavis would return to the colony.

The healers and scientists were still trying to identify both the narcotic and the poison that had killed him. The thought that someone had created more ways to get around the Vardarians' nanotech had everyone worried. Kade had been knocked out by one such substance. Now they knew of two more, and it appeared they were all connected to the corporations somehow.

Unfortunately, their best chance to link the attacks to the corporations hadn't produced much in the way of evidence. The explosion hadn't destroyed their mysterious suspect body completely, but what they recovered had created more questions. His DNA was not on record anywhere in the galaxy, and so far, facial recognition hadn't made a match. None of the ships docked had any record of him being on board, so how he got to the platform was yet another mystery. The one thing they did know was that among the fragments they recovered was a piece of tech no one had expected to find—a portion of a cellular lattice made from the suspect's own cells. They'd sent it to Nova Force for further study, but from what he understood, it was likely their suspect's consciousness hadn't died when his body had. He'd transferred himself away at the last minute. The Gray Men were fond of that tech, and that didn't bode well for the colony.

He didn't want to leave his post, but once the case

was over, he had to. It was necessary. And so today he would officially step down as Prince Tyran's *Naram T'kar*. Tyran had invited him to stay on as an advisor, a position he had happily accepted, though he was certain Skye and Phaedra had conspired to make that happen. It was not the way Vardarian culture worked, but as Skye kept reminding him, things were different here in Haven.

At the prince's request, he would make himself available to assist the new spymaster when one was appointed, but after today, his sole focus and duty would be Skye's happiness.

In the weeks since the incident on the orbital platform, the two of them had learned a great deal about each other, and every day he found something new to admire about his mate.

How could he have ever thought she was his punishment for failure? She was the most precious gift the universe and his ancestors had ever given him.

The guards at the door to the small throne room saw him coming and came to attention as he approached. This room didn't get much use, and neither did the elaborate garb he wore for the occasion. His boots were polished to a mirror finish and his pants had needlework in the colors of the royal house along the hem and side seams. His top was pure black while the collar was so encrusted with metal and gems that he could feel the weight of it across his shoulders. The one thing he'd never worn until recently was the *harani* that sat on his left biceps. The armband that announced his status as a mated male covered the tattoo that had once proclaimed his status as one of the *Naram T'kar*. The *harani* was made of two separate bands of precious metal, one gold and one black. The gold band had diamonds set into it, exactly as he'd requested. To him, they represented the light that Skye brought into his life.

The second band had contained a surprise. Skye had spoken to the forge masters and had them make a change of her own. The black metal had been inlaid with gold, creating a pattern that resembled the thorny *muhan* vine etched into his skin. It was perfect.

When he was within five steps of the door, the guards saluted and then opened the door to the throne room.

He expected the prince to be waiting for him alone. That was also a tradition. This was a solemn ceremony done in relative silence, with no one to witness the transfer of duty.

Since his replacement had not yet been found, no one would accept his symbol of office. Instead, he'd give it to the prince to hold on to until it was time to give it to another.

The moment he entered the room, he realized the prince was not alone. In fact, a small crowd stood along both flanking walls, carefully arranged so he hadn't seen them until he was inside.

He knew every one of them. Some were palace

staff. The entire leadership council was present along with several others, including Anya, Maggie, Shadow, and their mates.

Three figures moved to join Tyran beside his throne. Braxon and Phaedra took their places on either side of their prince, and Skye stopped several paces in front of the raised platform. She beamed at him with love and pride, confounding him even more.

"What is all this?" he asked, stopping when he was still several steps away from her.

"An intervention of a sort." Skye spoke through their private comm channel, so no one else heard what she said.

Then she smiled, held out her hand to him, and spoke aloud. "Trust me."

He almost managed not to grumble under his breath as she took his hand and led him to the foot of the throne.

Once there, he looked at Tyran, who sat on the simple throne he had chosen for himself and grinned down.

"Highness, I don't understand. I came here to resign as your *Naram T'kar.* You know that."

Tyran stood. "I do. However, I have decided to refuse your resignation."

Yardan gaped. That wasn't possible. It had to be this way.

Before he could say anything, Tyran cut him off with an upraised hand. "I've already heard your thoughts on this topic." His lips twitched. "Several times."

"We all have," Phaedra chimed in.

After a moment of general laughter, Tyran continued, "You've had your say. Now I will have mine. This colony was built to be a place to start over and escape the constraints of traditions so thick they were strangling us.

"I know it has always been the rule that a spymaster cannot have a mate, but you have been sent one. If the ancestors have chosen to bless you this way, who am I to argue with them?"

"But, Your Highness—"

His attempt to argue stopped when Skye squeezed his hand sharply. "No buts, Vin. Don't you see? The only one who believes you have to make a choice here is you. We took a vote, and we all agree that for once the universe is being generous. You don't have to give up anything. Not this time."

Speechless now, Yardan looked around the room. Everyone was smiling and nodding. These beings—no, his friends—all wanted this for him.

To quote his prince, who was he to argue?

He turned to Skye and drew her into his arms, no longer caring about tradition or protocol. "I would like it noted that if I had to choose, I would pick a life with you every time."

Her laughter was all the answer he needed. When his lips found hers, she kept laughing, her joy so contagious soon he had joined her, his kiss broken up by merry peals of laughter.

When he broke free, he kept Skye in his arms and looked up at Tyran. "I withdraw my resignation but with one caveat."

Skye looked up with surprise and Tyran arched one brow. "And what would that be, Spymaster?"

"Since we are already breaking with tradition, I'd like to change the way my office works. Oh, and hire more help. I can't take on the whole workload. After all, I have a mate to care for now."

Tyran nodded and then turned to wink at Skye. "Agreed. Would you like to tell him?"

Skye bounced on her toes. "Oh, yes." Then she laid both hands on his chest and beamed. "You don't need to worry about that. The prince has already hired someone to help you." She tapped her hand against his chest. "Me."

"You?" He pretended to think about that for a few seconds. "Alright. It makes sense. You get into trouble when I'm not around, so this should make it easier to do my job and keep you safe."

"*Me?* Ha! You don't need to keep me out of trouble. I'm the honey to your vinegar. You need *me*."

He leaned down and whispered his next words against her soft lips, every word coming straight from his heart. "I will always need you, my *ti'nar dani*."

Thank You for Reading Her Alien Spymaster

I hope you enjoyed Skye and Yardan's story.
Would you like to read a special bonus epilogue to this
story? Sign up for my newsletter here:
subscribepage.io/Bonuscontent

If you're looking for more Sci-fi romances like this one,
I invite you to explore the other books in the Drift
universe, which now Include Haven Colony, Nova
Force and the original Drift series.

ABOUT THE AUTHOR

Susan lives out on the Canadian west coast surrounded by open water, dear family, and good friends. She's jumped out of perfectly good airplanes on purpose and accidentally swum with sharks on the Great Barrier Reef.

If the world ends, she plans to survive as the spunky, comedic sidekick to the heroes of the new world, because she's too damned short and out of shape to make it on her own for long.

You can find out more about Susan and her books at:
www.susanhayes.ca